IMPRISONED IN IRAN

Love's Victory over Fear

DAN BAUMANN

YWAM
PUBLISHING
P.O. BOX 55787   SEATTLE, WA 98155

YWAM Publishing is the publishing ministry of Youth With A Mission. Youth With A Mission (YWAM) is an international missionary organization of Christians from many denominations dedicated to presenting Jesus Christ to this generation. To this end, YWAM has focused its efforts in three main areas: 1) Training and equipping believers for their part in fulfilling the Great Commission (Matthew 28:19). 2) Personal evangelism. 3) Mercy ministry (medical and relief work).

For a free catalog of books and materials write or call:

YWAM Publishing

P.O. Box 55787, Seattle, WA 98155

(425) 771-1153 or (800) 922-2143

www.ywampublishing.com

Imprisoned in Iran

Copyright ©2000 by Dan Baumann

10 09 08 07 06 05 04 03 02 01   10 9 8 7 6 5 4 3 2

Published by YWAM Publishing
P.O. Box 55787, Seattle, WA 98155

Unless otherwise noted, Scripture quotations in this book are taken from the Holy Bible, New International Version®, Copyright© 1973, 1978, 1984 by the International Bible Society. Used by permission of Zondervan Publishing House.

Verses marked KJV are taken from the King James Version of the Bible.

ISBN 1-57658-180-2

Printed in the United States of America.

Other International Adventures

Adventures in Naked Faith

Against All Odds

Dayuma: Life Under Waorani Spears

Living on the Devil's Doorstep

The Man with the Bird on His Head

Tomorrow You Die

Torches of Joy

Totally Surrounded

I dedicate this book to the Iranian people, whom I love and honor and long that they might know Jesus and how much He loves them!

From the bottom of my heart, I want to thank all of those who prayed and worked on my behalf to help get me out of prison. I am forever grateful for all you did!

Special thanks to Geoff and Janet Benge, who helped write this book. Your long hours, commitment to excellence, and most of all, friendship, have deeply blessed me!

Contents

Foreword

THE world needs more heroes. Real heroes, not the Hollywood type. We need men and women who aren't motivated by what they get out of something, but who are moved by their concern for others. We need heroes who really believe the world can be changed and who won't surrender to the prevailing cynicism and unbelief.

We need heroes who have one idea they believe can change the world and who are ready to act on it. These heroes are focused on the one thing that motivates them to the point of action. They have what Scripture calls "singleness of eye" and the "faith that produces obedience."

We also need heroes who are real, not the celluloid versions who say one thing and do another. Heroism is not about being perfect but about being ready. Ready to step up when it is time, ready to die for another person in a time of danger, ready at a moment's notice to take a stand for a friend. And ready to acknowledge one's weaknesses.

Dan Baumann is such a man. He is real, transparent, sometimes afraid, but always dreaming about the things that matter. Dan is not a realist, and I am glad. He lives for the dream. He has been captured by a compelling idea and is focused. He could say with Paul the Apostle, "This one thing I do!"

Dan is not perfect, but he will be the first person to admit that. What I love about Dan is that he bounces back. He faces his fears; though he gets overwhelmed by them like any ordinary human being, he "gets on the horse again" and again.

I watched Dan go through the prison experience he writes about in this book. I saw him up close and personal; I saw his fears and his pain. But I also saw that his compassion for friends still unknown to him was greater than his own fears. I saw Dan Baumann do the ultimate gut check and pass the test.

I strongly urge parents, grandparents, and youth pastors to get your kids to read this book. Better yet, read it to them. Talk about the lessons Dan learned, the dreams he dreamed.

Remember, all it takes is one person who believes—and then acts on—the idea that one compelling truth can change the world.

FLOYD McCLUNG

Metro Christian Fellowship
Kansas City, USA

ONE

Something We Hadn't Considered

Iran, January 1997

T H E tightness I had felt in my chest in the last hour had now turned into a nauseous knot of fear in my stomach. An oppressive silence hung in the air, but it did nothing to stop the pounding of my heart or cloak the terror I was experiencing.

As I walked silently beside my traveling companion, Glenn Murray, I noticed our captors did not appear to be armed, for which I was grateful. Though the temperature of Tehran's night air was dropping quickly, my shivering was not from the cold but from the fear of the unknown.

The buzz of rush-hour traffic had long since passed. Few vehicles drove by on the dimly lit street this late, and even fewer people ventured out on the narrow sidewalks. For a brief moment, I envisioned Glenn and me overpowering them and making a dash for freedom before the guards in front realized what was happening. But I was much too intimidated by the unexpected events of the previous few hours to attempt such a foolish James Bond escape move. Instead, I

compliantly followed my captors around the corner, where I saw three
ominous-looking vehicles parked at the curb. With a man on each side
of us, we were marched up to the middle vehicle, a beige-colored
Nissan Patrol that had dark curtains drawn across all but the front
window.

"Give me your glasses," demanded Mr. Akram, the only one who
had identified himself so far, as he opened the back door of the Patrol.

My heart sank as I pulled off my wire-rimmed spectacles. I had
worn glasses since I was fourteen years old and usually developed a
sickening headache when I didn't have them on.

Mr. Akram grabbed my glasses and put them in his front inside
coat pocket, then pulled out two black blindfolds. "Put these on," he
snapped, holding them out.

I took one last look at Glenn and then reluctantly pulled on my
blindfold. Once it was securely in place, a voice behind us yelled, "Get
in the car now!"

I felt myself being pushed roughly toward the edge of the curb.
Not wanting to trip and fall, I reached out and felt my way into the
back of the Nissan. Seconds later, Glenn tumbled in beside me.

I heard the doors of the vehicle slam shut and the locks click down.
A moment later the Nissan Patrol sped away from the curb.

"Are you okay?" I whispered to Glenn.

"So far. But I'd feel a lot better, Dan, if I knew where they were taking us and why."

"Yeah, me too," I replied, identifying with the same fear I heard
lurking behind Glenn's South African–accented words.

"Quiet," Mr. Akram yelled from the front seat.

Not wanting to antagonize them in any way, Glenn and I sat in
silence. As a gesture of support and encouragement, we clasped each
other's hand for the rest of the trip. As the vehicle continued to wind its
way through the streets of Tehran, my mind was buzzing with a number of possible scenarios, all of them frightening. Were we headed for
another meeting, a cold jail, or something far worse? A chill ran up my
spine when I realized no one except our captors knew where we were.
We were totally at their mercy and could easily wind up dead at the side
of the road with a bullet hole in the back of our heads. Since we didn't

have our passports, no one would know who we were or where we came from. Right then I lowered my head and offered a silent prayer, telling God I believed He was in control of every situation, even this one, though my silent words did little to settle my churning stomach.

Suddenly, the Nissan screeched to a halt. I could hear both front doors swing open, and Mr. Akram and the driver climbed out. Moments later the back door of the Nissan Patrol swung open. I awaited the order to get out, but it did not come. Instead, another man was pushed into the backseat and wedged beside us. Squinting out the side of my blindfold, I could see an Iranian man about fifty years old.

The doors to the vehicle slammed shut, and we were off once again. As the car raced through the streets, I wondered who the unfortunate man beside me was. What had an Iranian citizen done to incur the wrath of his own government? Could he possibly be a follower of Jesus or a renegade Muslim who refused to pray in public? Either case could bring serious consequences. Though I wished I knew his story, there was no way I could talk to him to satisfy my curiosity and take my mind off my own problems.

We drove on for about ten minutes, winding our way through narrow city streets, until finally we stopped. I heard large iron gates being swung open. The driver exchanged a few words with someone outside the vehicle, and then we drove on into what I surmised to be some sort of compound.

When the Nissan Patrol came to a halt this time, the three of us were ordered out. Over the course of the drive, I had managed to loosen my blindfold enough so I could see out the side and the bottom of it. While Mr. Akram was talking to someone, I turned my head and strained to catch a glimpse of where we were. Without my glasses, though, I could only make out a cream-colored concrete wall in the distance.

I felt a shove from behind and I stumbled forward, trying to regain my balance.

"Follow me," a voice hissed as a hand clamped around my wrist and began pulling me to the right.

My heart thumped wildly, and I could feel the bands of fear tightening their grip around my chest. I knew if I didn't do something, the wave of panic that was rising inside would overwhelm me, and I wouldn't be able to face whatever lay ahead. To help focus my mind, I began to count the number of stairs I was being led up. One… three…five…eight…ten. When we reached the top of the stairs, Glenn and I were led into a room.

"Take off your blindfolds," someone in the room commanded.

I blinked as my eyes adjusted to the bright fluorescent lights that hung from the grimy ceiling. Five men with menacing looks on their faces stood in the room staring at us. One was Mr. Akram, who from the very beginning of our capture a few hours ago was the only one to speak to us. The other four were dressed in crumpled uniforms. I saw no sign of the Iranian captive who had ridden with us. Much to my relief, Mr. Akram pulled my glasses from his inside coat pocket and handed them back to me. He watched as I put them on and then, without uttering a single word, turned and walked out of the room, leaving Glenn and me in the custody of the four men in uniforms.

As the door shut behind Mr. Akram, one of the uniformed men tore two black trash bags from a roll in the corner. "Here," he said, handing a bag to me, "take everything off and put it in here." He handed us two pieces of paper and a pencil and said, "Write a list of it as you go." He then grabbed some clothes from a pile in the corner and threw them at our feet. "Put these on," he snarled, obviously enjoying the power he had over us.

The man spoke in Farsi, which I understood, so I translated what he had said to Glenn. Together we began to strip off our belongings: watches, shirts, pants, shoes. Everything except our underwear was to be stuffed into the garbage bags.

After I had stripped off my clothes, I reached down and picked up the garments lying on the floor in front of me: a pair of long johns and a set of blue-and-white striped pajamas. Both were about two sizes too small for me, though I managed to squeeze myself into the pajamas and button up the coat. Grabbing the pencil and paper, I quickly made a list of everything I had taken off and then put the items into the garbage bag. I deliberately left my glasses on, hoping no one would take them from me again.

Once this humiliating ordeal was over, Glenn and I sat together on a hard and rickety wooden bench and waited. We talked quietly, though we were not much comfort to each other. I discovered that Glenn had not been interrogated for as long as I had been, and that most of the questions he was asked revolved around my being an American and what I was "really" doing in Iran.

Finally, after about ten minutes, the door opened and another guard marched into the room and threw two pairs of orange flip-flops down at our feet.

"Put them on," he commanded. "It's time to go."

By then my feet were beginning to go numb from the cold that seeped through the concrete floor. I slipped the flip-flops over my socks and stood up, wondering what was going to happen next. The guard motioned for Glenn and me to put our blindfolds back on. I slipped my glasses off and pulled the blindfold loosely over my head, all the while hoping no one would confiscate my glasses. Not being able to see clearly made me very uncomfortable and vulnerable. Unfortunately, one of our captors took them from me again.

A large hand clamped down around my wrist, and we were led from the room, down a flight of stairs, and into a gloomy basement. As I carefully made my way down the steps, I was puzzled by the sandbags I could feel piled on the left side of the stairs. I wondered if the building had once been used as a bomb shelter.

When we reached the bottom of the stairs, Glenn and I were separated. I could hear Glenn's flip-flops on the tile floor as he was taken to the right while I was led straight ahead before making a left turn. A red light glowed at the end of a drafty corridor. Just before I reached the light, the guard ordered me to halt. I heard a metal door being unlocked, and soon my escort shoved me forward. The heavy door swung shut and locked behind me with a disturbing finality. The panic I had felt earlier tried to resurface, and I silently prayed for God to give Glenn and me the strength to face this alone

I quickly pulled off the blindfold. I was in a cell about six feet wide and eight feet long. A scrappy piece of thin carpet lay on the tile floor, and an oil-heating radiator sat against the far wall. High in the top left corner was a small window with an old blanket stuffed in it. I presumed it was there to try to keep out the cold. Judging by the damp chill in the cell, it wasn't doing a very good job. Sighing, I turned and faced the locked metal door that held me captive. It had a mailboxlike opening about a foot up from the ground with no flap over it

I walked around the cell twice and then sat down on the threadbare carpet opposite the door, trying to control the conflicting emotions that coursed through me. I nervously ran my hands over my short-cropped reddish brown hair and tried to tell myself this was all a big mistake. The embassy would have Glenn and me out of here in a day at most, or would they? But I had my doubts about how much sway a foreign embassy really had in Iran. Slowly, I felt the crippling nausea of hopelessness mixed with fear and desperation begin to creep up from the pit of my stomach. I wrapped my arms around my knees and squeezed in a vain effort to comfort myself.

I was locked up alone in the basement of some jail in a country not known for its kindness to strangers, especially Americans like me. And even more disturbing, I had absolutely no idea why I was being held captive. What if the embassy couldn't get me out of this mess? What would happen then? As the waiting dragged on, I started to fear that I would just waste away in prison in Iran without anyone, including me, knowing why I was there. It had all seemed so simple when Glenn and I planned our trip from Turkmenistan to Iran several weeks before. We thought we had covered every detail. We had great plans that everything would go smoothly. We were wrong. We had never even considered the possibility of being thrown in jail.

TWO

The Man in the Park

THE ball hissed in the air as it narrowly cleared the net and hurtled toward me. I raced forward to intercept it, my right arm outstretched. I managed to get my racket under the ball and lob it up into a high arc. It sailed lazily over the head of my tennis partner, Glenn Murray, a tall blond South African. The ball went so high that Glenn decided it was not going to land inbound, so he didn't give chase. Somehow the spin on the ball brought it down just inside the baseline, and the game was mine.

"I don't believe it," Glenn said in his thick South African accent as he looked at the spot where the ball had landed. "Next time you won't be so lucky. Whew, it's hot. Let's have some water before we play another game, eh?"

"Sounds like a plan," I said as we plopped ourselves down on two white molded plastic chairs at the side of the court and opened our water bottles.

As we guzzled water, a European businessman decked out in a dark blue double-breasted suit with a red silk tie strolled by, carrying a leather briefcase. He was no doubt on his way to an important business meeting and probably assumed Glenn and I were relaxing after having attended one ourselves. He would have been partially right; we were relaxing. Glenn and I met together to play tennis each week at the Grand Turkmen Hotel. However, we were in Turkmenistan for very different reasons than the well-dressed businessman. Most foreigners who ventured this far into Central Asia came for one specific reason: to make as much money as they could off the vast oil reserves surrounding the Caspian Sea. Instead, we had come to Turkmenistan to share our faith in Jesus Christ. Glenn was a teacher at a language institute, and I was in the country on behalf of a Christian organization called Youth With A Mission (YWAM). Since 1988 I had worked with YWAM in a number of countries, including India, Afghanistan, and now Turkmenistan.

During my first week at El Camino Junior College in California in September 1983, when I began my studies in business and economics, I developed a deep interest in the Turkic people who inhabit a vast tract of Central Asia stretching all the way from Turkey to China. As I was praying in my dorm room at the beginning of that first semester, I felt God say He wanted me to go Ashgabad one day to share my faith. I had never heard of the place before, and when I looked it up on the map, I discovered it was the capital of the state known then as Turkmenia in the Soviet Union. While at first it sounded like a crazy and impossible idea, I knew that if it was truly God's will for me, then at the right time He would bring it to pass.

In 1991 Turkmenistan emerged as an independent nation after seventy years of military domination by the Soviet Union. The oppressive years of Soviet rule, though, had taken a serious toll on Turkmenistan's economy and its people. All forms of religion were suppressed, and the communists particularly brutalized the small community of Christians who lived there.

Turkmenistan sits in the middle of the Turkic world and is bordered to the south by Iran, to the west by the Caspian Sea, and to the north and east by Uzbekistan and Afghanistan respectively. While most of the Turkmen people live within Turkmenistan's borders, a number of them have spilled over into neighboring Afghanistan and Iran.

When an opportunity finally arose to go to Turkmenistan, I jumped at the chance. As a result, thirteen years after first hearing God speak to me about Ashgabad, I was living there. My sole reason for coming to Turkmenistan was to share the love of Jesus with the Turkmen people. To effectively pursue that goal, I was trying to make contacts and search out practical ways Christians from other countries could help Turkmen Christians and encourage them to reach out with the Good News to their fellow Turkmen, most of whom were Muslims.

"So how are things going, eh?" Glenn asked as the man in the business suit disappeared from our view. Glenn ended most of his sentences with "eh." It was a kind of verbal question mark that indicated he wanted a response.

"Fine," I replied. "I have a couple of local people who are interested in doing a Bible study with me. My Russian language studies are going well, too."

While Turkmen was the official language spoken in Turkmenistan, Russian remained the most commonly used language in the larger cities. For this reason I had set about learning Russian as soon as I could. A friend of mine named Sergei had agreed to be my tutor on a regular basis. Sergei was in his midtwenties, and I spent several hours with him each day learning the difficult language.

Learning Russian turned out to be more of a challenge than I had imagined. I found it even harder than learning Farsi, which I had learned while living in Afghanistan. I had gone to Kabul, Afghanistan, in 1988 to work as the administrator of a hospital, putting to good use the business/economics degree I had earned at Wheaton College in Illinois. I remained in Afghanistan until 1993. As a result of my time there, I spoke fairly fluent Farsi. Along with Farsi, I also spoke Swedish, which my Scandinavian mother had taught me from birth.

"The people here in Turkmenistan are pretty open to the Good News at present. I've been asked more questions than ever at school about what it means to be a Christian," Glenn said, running his hands through his wavy blond hair. He took a deep breath and gulped some more water from his bottle before continuing on. "Lately I've been wishing I could do something to contact the Turkmen in Iran, eh."

"That's interesting," I said as I took off my glasses and mopped my forehead with a towel, "because I've been thinking about the same thing lately."

A broad smile lit up Glenn's face. "Is that right?" he said. "You know, they must be some of the most isolated people on earth. I hear you can get the death penalty in Iran for owning a satellite dish or watching a Western movie, and certainly for converting to Christianity."

"You're right about that, Glenn," I nodded, "but there are effective means of presenting the Good News to Iranian Muslims. You just have to go about it the right way."

Glenn's green eyes were fixed firmly on me, so I carried on. "I visited Iran two and a half years ago. It was an interesting experience. Everywhere I went, I discovered people who were open to hearing the Good News, especially if someone talked to them in their language and understood some of their cultural ways. If we could get Turkmen Christians to somehow mingle with the Turkmen in Iran and present the Good News to them in their own language, amazing things could happen."

"That's the answer!" Glenn blurted out, the corners of his face curling up into a tight, animated grin. "Do you think there's something we could do to help it come about?"

"I don't know," I replied. "Recently I've had this strange desire to go back into Iran and try to make some meaningful contacts. Maybe something could work out. We'd make a good pair. You speak Turkmen and I speak Farsi. We'd need Farsi for all of the official stuff and Turkmen if we were able to contact some Turkmen people."

"Yeah, but what about your being an American?" Glenn asked. "I mean they're not exactly putting out a welcome mat for Americans in Iran."

I smiled. "I'm not just a regular American guy from Southern California!" I said with mock indignation. "My parents were immigrants—Mom is from Sweden, and Dad is from Switzerland. Thanks to Dad I have dual citizenship. When I'm in this part of the world, I travel on my Swiss passport. That's how I was able to get into Iran the last time, and how I got around so freely."

"Let's pray about it and see how we feel next week, eh?" Glenn suggested.

The following week Glenn and I met again for our regular round of tennis at the hotel. Between games we sat and discussed the possibility of going to Iran on sort of a reconnaissance trip for future mission possibilities. We both felt it was still a good idea, though some obstacles had come into sharp focus during the week, the biggest one being that we had no contacts inside Iran. Without any contacts it seemed very unlikely that we would be able to get off the "tourist track" and meet Turkmen people. After talking some more, we decided that if God sent a contact our way, we would take that as His green light to proceed with the next step of our plan. Throughout my life God has often given me specific confirmations like this to indicate I was on the right path.

Surprisingly, we didn't have to wait long. The very next afternoon I was sitting in Second Park, not far from my drab apartment on the north side of Ashgabad. Most afternoons Sergei and I would go to the park so I could practice Russian. After an afternoon of battling to get my mind around a new set of verbs, I decided to head for home.

I always enjoyed a leisurely stroll back through the park on my way to catch the bus to my apartment. Not only was my Russian lesson over for the day, but the gentle breeze that rustled through the trees and across the park provided a welcome reprieve from Ashgabad's normally oppressive heat.

As I approached the main gate to the park, I spotted a man sitting on a bench. Nothing in particular distinguished him from any other man in the park. Like most of the older men, he had a long beard and wore a dull brown suit over a white dress shirt, the virtual uniform of upper-class men in Turkmenistan. Yet there was something different about this man, which I was immediately drawn to. I slowed my brisk pace, wondering what I should do. I didn't speak Turkmen, and I certainly didn't feel confident enough in Russian to hold a meaningful conversation with a stranger. I also thought it was unlikely he spoke Swedish or English. Logic told me to keep walking toward the bus stop. I had no reason to try to strike up a conversation with the man. Yet something deep inside told me God had him there for a special appointment, so I followed the nudge I felt.

I walked over to the bench where the man was sitting, nodded politely, and sat down beside him. He nodded back and moved the newspaper that lay between us. I felt his eyes survey my Levi jeans, bottle green Eddie Bauer shirt, and loafers. It was obvious that my Western attire along with my six-foot frame and reddish brown hair immediately gave me away as a foreigner.

"Do you speak English?" I asked him in English. He shot me a puzzled look. It was obvious he understood no English.

I tried again, this time in Farsi. "Farsi meifamein?" (Do you speak Farsi?) I asked.

"Bale," he replied to my surprise and delight.

"Salam allekum, chetowrastein?" (How are you?) I asked, offering a firm handshake.

"Khubam shoma chetowrid?" he replied, shaking my hand vigorously.

"My name is Dan Baumann, and I am from America," I continued in Farsi.

"And I am Raheem from Iran," the man replied.

I could scarcely believe I was having this conversation. I was probably sitting next to the only Iranian in the park, and he was warm and open and friendly. I tried to appear casual as I talked to him, but my mind was racing with excitement and a host of questions. Could he be the contact God had for Glenn and me in Iran? We chatted away in Farsi. Although there were some differences in words between the Farsi I had learned in Afghanistan and the Farsi spoken in Iran, nonetheless we managed to learn quite a lot about each other. I told Raheem about my life growing up in America, and in turn he told me he was a Turkmen, and a cleric, a Muslim religious leader in Iran. We also talked about our families. After twenty minutes of conversation, though, I could not hold back any longer. I blurted out how Glenn and I were thinking about making a trip to Iran. "Do you think that would be a good idea?" I asked.

Raheem's eyes lit up. "Of course, you must come!" he exclaimed. "I insist. You will be my family's honored guests the whole time." As if to solidify the arrangement, he pulled out a small notepad from his jacket pocket and began to scribble a note. "Here," he said after a few moments, ripping the top page from the pad. "If you have any trouble obtaining your visa, give this note to someone at the Iranian embassy. I have written my address on the top. You must come to visit me. I will be looking forward to you and your friend coming."

We talked for a few moments more, and then Raheem said he had to leave. We stood and shook hands, and then I watched him turn and walk off through the park gate. As I stood there holding the note Raheem had given me, I was amazed at what had just transpired. That short meeting seemed to be the tangible evidence that God definitely wanted Glenn and me to visit Iran. What else would prompt a total stranger who was a Muslim leader to invite a young Christian man from the United States to come and visit him as his "honored guest" in his home in Iran—a country not tolerant of Christianity or Westerners?

I could hardly wait to tell Glenn the news. The following evening I excitedly made my way across town to his apartment. I told him all about meeting Raheem in the park and how he had extended an invitation to visit him in Iran. Glenn also had some good news. Convinced the trip was the right thing to do, he had told a few people about our plans. As a result, one of the other foreign teachers in the city wanted to accompany us on the trip. The man's name was Greg, and he was twenty years old. Glenn told me Greg spoke fluent Russian, which would be a great asset on the trip. On the downside, though, he was an American, which meant he might encounter some difficulties obtaining an entry visa for Iran. Glenn also had another man who wanted to go with us. He was a Turkmen Christian named Mustafa, and he had a second cousin in Iran he wanted to visit.

With Greg's language ability and a Turkmen who had a contact in Iran, Glenn and I agreed it would be helpful if both men accompanied us. To avoid any unnecessary suspicions at the Iranian embassy, we decided it would be best if all of our papers did not become entangled as we applied for our entry visas. We applied for our visas several days before the other two men so the officials at the embassy would not suspect we were traveling as a group. Some friends had told us that the Iranian officials often got suspicious when groups of foreigners wanted to travel to Iran together.

The next night in my apartment, I sat down to fill out the application for an Iranian entry visa. I had filled out plenty of similar documents before, since I had visited over fifty countries in all my travels. The Iranian application seemed basically the same as all the others. The first question read, "Place of Birth." I wrote down Santa Monica,

California, United States of America. And then I added my date of birth in response to the second question.

In answer to the third question, which asked what my citizenship was, I wrote, "Swiss." This was true because the Swiss government had a policy that anyone who had a parent born in Switzerland could be registered as a Swiss citizen and carry a passport. I knew the Iranians would have no difficulty understanding the concept of belonging to your father's place of origin. In Eastern cultures the physical place where your mother gave birth to you is not nearly as important as the place where your father's family has lived for generations.

The next question caused me to ponder a bit, though. Do you hold dual citizenship with any other country? I knew if I answered yes and wrote down the United States, I ran the risk of having my visa turned down. But I couldn't write no. That would be a lie. Finally I decided to leave the space blank. It was obvious to anyone reading the application carefully that I was also an American, since I had been born there.

The following day I took the application to the Iranian embassy, a rectangular beige building located in the heart of town and decorated with blue tiles that bore various slogans in artistic Persian script. The inside was spotlessly clean, and large potted plants were arranged so as to mark off a large square area in front of a polished wooden counter. The whole place seemed to have an air of efficiency and décor that seemed unusual for Turkmenistan. There was no line at the counter, so I walked straight over and nervously handed my visa application to a consular officer. The man glanced over the form casually and asked where exactly I wanted to go in Iran. I slid my hand into the pocket of my Levi's and pulled out the slip of paper Raheem had given me in the park. The official's eyebrows rose slightly as he read the note and then folded it and handed it back to me. He scribbled some notation in pencil on top of the application form and told me to come back in two weeks. By then, he assured me, my paper work would be processed, and I would know if my visa had been approved.

Two weeks later to the day, on a crisp fall afternoon, I made my way back to the Iranian embassy. I was nervous as I approached the counter and told the official I was there to check on my visa application. To my surprise, good news awaited me. My visa had been approved. I hurried off to tell Glenn that we would soon be off on our trip.

THREE

On the Border

ON Thursday, December 19, 1996, Glenn and I met outside the Iranian embassy for one final visit before collecting our visas. All that remained was to pay a U.S.$50 fee and have the visa stamped into our passports.

We stood together outside the imposing building for a moment, talking about all that had happened in the last few weeks.

"It's bad news about Mustafa, eh?" Glenn said. "There's no way he's going to get his travel documents before next Thursday."

I nodded my head slowly in agreement. Observing Mustafa trying to get permission to travel around inside Iran was both frustrating and disheartening. As a citizen of Turkmenistan, he did not need a visa to enter Iran. But in order to move around once he was there, he needed official travel documents granting him permission to go to the particular places he intended to visit. To obtain the necessary permission, he needed to tell the Iranian authorities whom he would be visiting and where he would be staying in each place.

"He's been getting the royal runaround," continued Glenn, gesturing with his head toward the door of the Iranian embassy. "They told him it would be a month or more before he would know if he had been granted permission to travel inside the country."

"That's too bad," I said sincerely. "Mustafa would have been a great asset on the trip." Frankly, the thought of not having him along as guide and interpreter made me a little nervous. I was beginning to wonder how successful we would be at making contact with other Turkmen inside Iran without him.

We had also just learned that Greg would not be coming with us either. He had submitted his application for a visa twice. Each time he went back to check on it, he received the same swift reply, a red stamp on his application marking it "denied." Since we had all applied for our Iranian visas at the same office, it seemed obvious to us that being an American was what counted Greg out. I thought it was a bit strange that no one at the embassy questioned my Swiss citizenship, when I was born in the United States. But I wasn't too worried about it. The last time I had gone into Iran I had used my Swiss passport, and I hadn't run into any problems at the border.

As usual, the Iranian embassy was a model of brisk efficiency. Once inside, Glenn and I handed over our fees, and the clerk stamped an Iranian entry visa into each of our passports. The visa allowed us to enter Iran by Thursday, December 26, one week away.

Everything seemed set except for one detail. Glenn still needed official permission to travel to Iran from the leader of the group he served with as a teacher. The weekend came and went, and he still had not received final approval to go. Christmas Day arrived, though it was just another day in Muslim-controlled Turkmenistan, and still Glenn had not heard any reply. I began to get a little anxious. If we did not enter Iran soon, our visas would expire. Finally, late in the afternoon, I heard a tap on my apartment door. When I opened it, there stood Glenn, grinning from ear to ear.

"I've finally been given permission to go," he announced.

A surge of conflicting emotions ran through me at the good news. Of course I was delighted to finally know we were going, but I also felt a tinge of dread mixed with it. I decided that the apprehension probably had something to do with the fact that we would be crossing the border into Iran via a less traveled and more isolated northern route, one not used much by Westerners. Who could anticipate the difficulties we might encounter at the border?

Inside the apartment Glenn chatted on excitedly as I threw my belongings for the trip into a maroon leather bag. I didn't need much, just a couple of changes of clothes, sleeping bag, camera, notebook, Bible, and wallet. I stuffed U.S.$300 into my wallet, which I decided would be plenty for the journey. As long as we kept off the main tourist trail, our expenses shouldn't be that great. In fact, I was still shocked at how far a few dollars would go once converted to the local currency.

After I had gathered all my gear together, we set out across town for Glenn's apartment to pick up his things. He lived closer to the bus depot, from where we would depart early the following morning on the hundred-twenty-mile trip from Ashgabad across the border to Mashad, Iran's second largest city.

We stopped at a local restaurant for dinner on the way and arrived at the apartment after the sun had gone down. I stretched out my sleeping bag on the floor and prepared to turn in for the night. We had a long day of travel ahead of us, and I wanted to get as much sleep as possible before setting out on our journey.

"What should we take, eh? That's the next thing to figure out," Glenn said as I arranged my sleeping bag. He reached for a book from the shelf behind his threadbare sofa. It was a Christian book written in Persian. "What do you think? Should we take some with us?" he asked.

His question caught me a little off guard. We were going on an exploratory trip into Iran to see if we could forge some links between Turkmen Christians and their Muslim kin on the other side of the border. I hadn't given any thought to smuggling Christian literature into Iran as well. "I'm all for getting Christian materials into Iran," I began, "but being caught with a pile of books like that could land us in jail."

Glenn nodded.

"The question is, on this trip are we supposed to be smuggling literature into Iran or simply making contacts so Turkmen Christians can go back after us and share the Good News?"

"Good point," Glenn admitted, "but it seems a shame not to take something with us. What about this?" he asked, pulling a copy of the *Jesus* movie dubbed in Persian from the shelf.

I thought about my previous trip to Iran for a moment. "They didn't body search me the last time," I offered. "I suppose we could take that one thing and keep it on one of us at the border."

A few minutes later I was curled up in my sleeping bag on the floor. However, despite being tired, sleep did not come easily. While Glenn snored peacefully in bed, I tossed and turned on the thin carpet. By now the food I had eaten for dinner had become a burning hot lump in the pit of my belly. So instead of sleeping, I played over in my head various scenarios of what might lie ahead for us in Iran.

As the night dragged on, I could hear cars and the occasional roar of a bus as they sped by on one of Ashgabad's main thoroughfares a block and a half away. Closer, the howl of a dog set off a round of riotous barking and howling across the area. Then at about 3 A.M. the door to a neighboring apartment slammed, and a volley of yelling erupted between a man and a woman.

Finally, at 4 A.M. I drifted off to sleep, only to be awoken an hour later by the annoying buzz of Glenn's alarm clock. I dragged myself out of the sleeping bag with difficulty and rubbed my eyes as they slowly adjusted to the bare incandescent bulb that lit the living room from above. There was no need to get dressed, for I had slept in my clothes. I simply ran my hands over them to smooth out a few of the wrinkles. I didn't feel like breakfast. I could still feel dinner from the night before in my stomach. And there was no time to brew any tea. We needed to be out of the apartment in fifteen minutes, so I headed for the bathroom to splash some cold water on my face.

Before we set out, Glenn and I took several minutes to pray together. We asked God to bless our trip and help us cross the border safely without any incidents and to make friends with the Iranians we met along the way.

Finally, it was time to leave for the bus station. I pulled on my jacket and then slipped the *Jesus* video into the inside pocket. "Can you notice it?" I asked.

"Looks normal to me," Glenn replied, shaking his head at the same time.

"Okay, we're out of here," I said, pulling the door to Glenn's apartment open.

Glenn hoisted a small backpack onto his back and followed me, turning off the light and locking the door behind him.

Outside in the predawn dark, we saw only a few people out on the streets. We walked the block and a half to one of Ashgabad's main streets. We didn't need to worry about finding a taxi. Almost any driver in Turkmenistan will pull over if you flag them down. For a few dollars they are usually more than happy to take you anywhere you want to go. This morning we didn't even need to flag down a driver. Before we reached the curb, an old, dilapidated Russian Volga pulled up alongside us. The driver, a middle-aged man with graying hair and a bulbous red nose, leaned over and wound down the window.

"Do you need a ride somewhere?" he asked politely in Turkmen.

"Yes, thank you," Glenn replied, reaching over and heaving open the back door of the old gray automobile.

Ten minutes later the driver deposited us safely at Ashgabad's main bus station. I walked over under a streetlight and looked at my watch. It was exactly 6 A.M. There were three groups of people standing around in the darkness. Glenn and I joined the group waiting under the sign that read "Mashad."

Besides us, a dozen other people were waiting for the bus. As we stood there, I studied them quietly. Two women were dressed in their traditional long dark dresses with colorful scarves tied around their heads. Next to them stood a group of young men carrying a variety of plastic goods, bound together with twine.

Before we had time to strike up a conversation with any of the members of the group, a battered, grimy white bus belching black smoke lumbered to a halt in front of us, and everyone climbed aboard. No sooner had we finished stowing our belongings under the seat or on the rickety luggage rack above than the driver ground the gears and the bus rumbled off, leaving a cloud of smoke trailing behind.

As we wound through the streets of Ashgabad, the first ribbons of dawn draped themselves across the stirring city. By the time we finally left the city behind, the sun had risen fully.

It was only thirty miles from there to the border, but it took an hour and a half to cover the distance. Soon after leaving the city we began to climb the Kōpetdag Mountains that separated Turkmenistan and Iran. The diesel engine of the bus groaned and labored for every mile we covered. At the dismal speed we were traveling, I guessed it would be well after dark before we made it to Mashad.

The slow trip, though, gave us time to get to know our fellow passengers. Most were small-time business people on their way to Iran to trade plastic goods and bolts of black cotton fabric that were wrapped in brown paper. One of the men explained that the fabric was used to make the full-face veils that Iranian women wore in public.

Our fellow passengers were equally curious about us, wanting to know why two Westerners were riding on the bus with them. Glenn explained that we were visiting Iran to see if we could set up trading arrangements for some of our Turkmen friends. This news got the young men all very excited, and they began offering us suggestions as to how we might proceed.

After about an hour, an ominous quiet settled over the bus. People began digging around in their bags for their passports and other travel documents. It was obvious from their actions that we were approaching the border. I felt in my jacket pocket for my passport. It was safely tucked in beside the *Jesus* video.

The bus lurched to a stop at a small checkpoint in the middle of nowhere. A Turkmen official climbed aboard and began checking to see if anyone on the bus was trying to export illegal materials. A few items were confiscated amidst a spate of heated words, and twenty minutes later we were back on the road.

Our next stop, though, turned out to be a much more sinister-looking place. We rounded a sharp turn in the road, and a line of barbed wire came into view. I craned my neck to see a small sand-block structure at the side of the road surrounded by soldiers in green uniforms clasping AK-47s. The driver shifted gears and guided the bus to a halt in front of the structure.

No one on the bus spoke a word as two soldiers climbed aboard and barked out orders in Russian. "Get out," they yelled. "And bring your luggage."

We were still on the Turkmenistan side of the border, so I did not worry too much. I was sure it would be a routine check to ensure that the Turkmen on the bus had the proper permission to exit Turkmenistan and enter Iran.

Everyone moved at once, eager to comply with the soldiers' demands. I pulled my bag down from the rack above my head and joined the stream of people clambering off the bus.

A bitter cold wind whipped around my legs as I exited. I found myself wishing I had put on a pair of long johns beneath my Levi's. And a warm hat would have been nice, too, as my ears went instantly numb from the frigid cold that blew down off the mountains.

"They're not really open for the day yet," commented one of our fellow passengers as we all huddled together for warmth outside the building. In a low voice the passenger added, "You watch when they get started on the bus. You haven't seen anything like it."

Fifteen minutes later I understood what he meant. A group of soldiers descended on the bus like a swarm of hungry ants. They removed the side panels and beat the tires and wheel arches with batons. They even unscrewed the light fixtures and checked behind them.

"They're looking for drugs, though I've never been on a bus where they found any," the friendly passenger told Glenn and me.

Soon the door to the gray sand-block building opened, and everyone picked up their belongings and began to form a line. Glenn and I followed, taking our place at the back of the line of people that soon snaked in a semicircle along the wall of the building and in the door. After about ten minutes, the line had moved enough so that Glenn and I could see what was happening inside. One by one we watched as our fellow passengers produced their travel documents and then placed their bags on a long, narrow table. A soldier looked over each person's papers, and once he was satisfied they were in order, he signaled for two other soldiers to search their bags thoroughly. They not only emptied each bag but also patted down the outside and felt for any hidden compartments that might contain contraband items.

After watching the procedure repeated several times, I began to get nervous. If the border guards were this meticulous on the Turkmenistan side of the border, how much more thoroughly would the Iranians search us? I felt the bulge of the *Jesus* video in my jacket pocket and began to fear that some guard would notice it and ask what it was. "I don't know what'll happen if I get caught with this video," I whispered to Glenn.

"Nor do I," he said. "These guards are sure thorough, eh? What do you think we should do?"

"I think we should get rid of the tape, and the sooner the better," I said. "It's not worth risking our whole trip for it."

Glenn nodded in agreement. "How?" he asked.

"Leave it to me," I said, sounding more confident than I really was. I looked around for somewhere to dump the video. Nothing looked too promising inside the building. I felt the eyes of every guard boring into my back. *God, please help me here! What should I do?* Suddenly an idea came to me. I couldn't see a bathroom in the building. I looked out beyond the parking lot and spotted a small outhouse off in the distance.

"Glenn," I whispered, "tell them I need to go to the bathroom and I don't speak Turkmen."

Glenn stepped forward and addressed the closest soldier. The soldier frowned and mumbled something under his breath before motioning for me to step forward. He marched me to the outhouse.

Once inside the rickety wooden structure, I shut and bolted the door. I had mixed feelings as I slipped the video out of my jacket pocket. On the one hand, I was a bit disappointed in myself. I wasn't another Brother Andrew, daringly smuggling materials across hostile borders. Yet I told myself there was no point in taking unnecessary risks that would jeopardize the whole purpose of our coming to Iran. Smuggling wasn't the focus of our trip. Making good contacts for future visits was the reason we had come.

The video made a loud noise as it hit the bottom of the outhouse pit. With the video gone, I felt much better as I left the outhouse and headed back to join Glenn and the rest of the passengers from the bus. Glenn was inside now and nearly to the table. As I slipped back in line behind him, I subtly gave him the thumbs up.

When it was my turn, I handed over my Swiss passport and placed my bag on the table. The soldier thumbed through the pages of the passport until he came to the freshly stamped entry visa for Iran. He looked at it, then handed the passport back to me. The two other soldiers gave my bag a cursory search and then waved me on.

Glenn and I waited beside the wall on the far side of the room as the rest of the passengers stuffed their belongings back into their bags.

A few of them were arguing and yelling with the soldiers, while several of the men, who seemed to be old hands at crossing the border, were wheeling and dealing their way to compromises with the guards.

Finally, after about two hours of waiting, our bus was ready for the continuation of the journey to Mashad, and we all climbed back aboard.

We drove on for several miles until a metal fence came into view. Beyond the fence I could see a building with Persian writing painted on it and an Iranian flag flapping in the stiff breeze above. After passing through a checkpoint, the bus pulled to a halt in front of the building.

Once again we were ordered off the bus and then led inside single file to pass through Iranian customs. As I walked through the door, my nervousness quadrupled. An almost palpable feeling of being under total control swept over me. We had now entered a country where, officially, the central message of our faith was not welcome and even snuffed out at every opportunity.

As I turned to take one last look at Turkmenistan, I noticed a white Toyota van cross the border. It was unusual to see such a modern vehicle in this part of the world, and I strained my eyes to see who was inside. I could see two men, and I had the distinct feeling I had seen one of them before, though I couldn't remember where. Finally, it came to me, and with it a sense of foreboding. One of them was the young man from the Iranian embassy in Ashgabad who had issued my entry visa. *What a strange coincidence that he's right behind our bus,* I thought before diverting my attention back to the building we had just entered.

I looked around at the room. It was large and stark and decorated with a wall-to-ceiling portrait of Ayatollah Khomeini painted in harsh colors on black fabric. We had plenty of time to study the portrait as we waited for over an hour to be processed by immigration officials. As usual, there were more forms to fill out, but the process went smoothly. After having the date of entry stamped into my passport, I was led into the customs hall, where more paperwork awaited. Again I encountered no problems, much to my relief. The customs officer barely looked at my bag. Soon I was sitting back on the bus beside Glenn.

Other passengers also began to drift back onto the bus. As the man in the seat behind us loaded his luggage up onto the overhead rack, he glanced at Glenn's passport and muttered to him in Turkmen.

With a puzzled look Glenn handed the man his passport. I watched as he thumbed carefully through its pages. Soon he and Glenn were engaged in a flurry of animated conversation.

After a couple minutes Glenn turned to me with a look of dismay. "He says we're not finished yet, eh? There's a slip of paper that records how much money we brought into the country that needs to be signed. We don't have one, and he says it's very important."

Glenn and I clambered off the bus again. After asking one of the other passengers, we found where the slip was issued and got in line. The line moved slowly, but eventually we got to the front, where an official asked us to show him our money supply. I pulled out the U.S.$300 from my wallet and waited as the official counted the money carefully. When he was finished, he took a pink slip of paper and recorded the amount. Next he stamped over the writing and then placed a piece of scotch tape over it all. I assumed it was the Iranian way of making a document tamper proof.

"This paper is very important," Glenn said, relaying what the official was telling him. "It will be hard to get out of the country without this."

I certainly didn't want any trouble when it came time to leave Iran, so I folded the paper neatly and tucked it into the back of my passport.

"Yes!" I exclaimed to Glenn as we got back on the bus for what we thought was the last time. "We've made it." A wave of relief swept through me. The worst was behind us. We had been issued permits that allowed us to travel freely inside Iran. In two weeks we would be crossing the border back into Turkmenistan—hopefully with several valuable contacts for our Turkmen friends.

FOUR

On to Tehran

W E had only gone a few miles when the bus was flagged down at yet another checkpoint just across the border. This one was manned by Iranian policemen who ordered us all off the bus. I began to wonder if a single day would be enough for us to get to Mashad! Once everyone was off the bus, we all stood in line parallel to it as one policeman checked travel papers and the other searched each person. When the policemen got to me, they made me take off my jacket and show them every scrap of paper I had in my pockets. I was very glad I no longer had the videotape on me.

After looking at my passport and checking my visa, the policeman turned to the man beside me and began peppering him with questions in Turkmen while his colleague patted me down, searching for hidden contraband. As the policeman talked to the Turkmen passenger, he kept looking back at Glenn and me. I was sure they were talking about us, but I had no idea what was being said.

Finally Glenn whispered, "He's asking the passenger about who we are and what we're doing on the bus."

I smiled and waited anxiously. Eventually the policeman seemed satisfied with the answers he received and moved on down the line checking the rest of the passengers' travel papers.

After checking everyone's papers, the police then turned their attention to the bus. Like the soldiers on the Turkmenistan side of the border, they were thorough and methodical in their search for anything illegal.

As two policemen crawled under the back of the bus in the course of their search, one of the passengers said something aloud in Turkmen. The crowd burst into laughter.

Glenn translated for me. "He said, 'What are you looking for? Chickens?'"

I laughed, too, and although I didn't get the joke, it felt good to be doing something to break the tension in the air. After all the searches we had been through together, a camaraderie had quickly developed among the passengers.

An hour later the police finished their search, and we were back on the bus winding our way through scattered mountain villages. The slow pace gave me ample opportunity to study the tiny Iranian communities we drove through. I was surprised at how different the architecture was from the gray, multistoried buildings of Ashgabad. The small mud-brick homes reminded me of the adobe-brick dwellings of Mexican villages. Many of the towns had colorful bazaars that buzzed with people buying and selling wares. At the sight of so many people, I couldn't help but wonder who would tell them the Good News. In village after village we passed, no one had ever heard about the love of Jesus. I counted it a real privilege to be here, and an excitement began to grow in my heart. I was finally in Iran and would soon be out meeting the local people.

It was late in the afternoon when I spotted what I assumed was Mashad off in the distance. The city seemed to glimmer in the fast fading light of dusk, and I anxiously looked forward to the end of an arduous day of traveling. But before we reached our destination, we had to stop once more in the outer suburbs.

The sun had finally set when the bus swung into an open market area illuminated by dim streetlights and ground to a halt. The driver muttered a few sentences in Turkmen before climbing out of his bus.

"We'll be here for about an hour," Glenn informed me. "We might as well climb out and get something to eat."

I nodded in eager agreement. I hadn't eaten anything since the night before, and suddenly I became aware of the gnawing hunger pangs in my stomach.

As Glenn and I stepped out of the bus, we were instantly surrounded by men who urged us to exchange our money with them.

"Dollars?" they asked, pressing close to us. "You got dollars?"

We walked a few feet from the bus, and then I reached for my wallet. I pulled out five twenty-dollar bills and held them out to the man standing nearest me. He smiled and held up a handful of *rial*, the local currency.

I counted the wad of dirty bills he held out and quickly did the math in my head. The exchange rate seemed fair, so I nodded my head and swapped my money for his. I folded the rial and stuffed them into my wallet alongside my remaining dollars.

"How about some kebabs for dinner, eh?" Glenn suggested after the transaction was done.

"Sounds like a plan," I said. "I'm famished."

We made our way to an open cooking area with a few folding chairs scattered around it. The owner showed an immediate interest in having foreigners for customers. We gave the man our order, and soon we were both handed platters piled high with lamb kebabs served on a bed of fluffy white rice. After the long day of travel we had endured, I would have eaten anything, but the kebabs were delicious and so was the rice. The meal wasn't at all greasy like the rice they served in Turkmenistan.

We also ordered some hot sweet tea and were still sitting drinking it when we heard the now familiar honk of the bus horn announcing its departure. It was time for the final leg of our journey.

Our fellow passengers drifted back to the bus, some carrying plates of food and mugs of drink, which they proceeded to eat as we wound our way through the narrow streets to the center of Mashad. As I stared out the window, I realized we would soon have to think about some type of lodging.

"Hey, Glenn," I said. "Ask your friend if he knows of a cheap place where foreigners can stay."

Glenn launched into Turkmen, and after several minutes of conversation, he turned back to me. "He says four of them are going to spend the night in a local boardinghouse. They said we are welcome to go there with them. It costs about a dollar a night. The place has beds and a common bathroom for everyone. What do you think?"

"It sounds okay to me," I said, grateful for the cheap lodging. I was even more grateful that some of the men trusted us enough to invite us to go along with them. Their friendliness gave me hope that we could make some good contacts while we were here.

After a few minutes, the bus finally pulled up outside a large dilapidated hotel. Several passengers disembarked, and our new friends nodded for us to get off, too. It was about a half-mile walk from there to the boardinghouse.

As one of the Turkmen talked to the man at the counter, I looked around. The boardinghouse was pretty much as our Turkmen friend had described it. The six of us were shown into a single room filled with beds. It took me only a couple of minutes to get ready to turn in. I brushed my teeth, took off my shoes, and claimed the bed closest to the wall. I rolled up a pair of jeans into a makeshift pillow and lay down. Even though I had been sitting on the bus for most of the day, I was completely exhausted. As I thought about all the places we had stopped at along the way, I quickly did some mental arithmetic. No wonder I felt so tired. It had taken sixteen grueling hours to go 120 miles. That averaged out to seven and a half miles an hour! Within minutes I was sound asleep.

Shafts of pale sunlight streaking in the window awoke me the next morning. It took a minute or two as I rubbed the sleep from my eyes to remember where I was. I glanced at my watch. It was nearly 7 A.M., and our four Turkmen friends were already up. Glenn was snoring loudly beside me, and I decided not to wake him. I got up quietly and went off in search of breakfast and then took a walk around Mashad.

I arrived back at the boardinghouse at 10 A.M. and found Glenn sitting in the room happily chatting to ten Turkmen. I recognized the four men from the bus and assumed the others were the business contacts they had come to see. I smiled, sat down, and joined them. Although I could not understand what they were saying, I got the impression they were discussing ways Glenn and I could meet some of their countrymen in Iran who might want to trade with people in Turkmenistan. We hadn't been here even a day, and it seemed that we were having success. I smiled and silently thanked God, asking Him to continue blessing our endeavors.

Around 11 A.M. another man entered the room carrying a bag. He opened the bag and spread a tablecloth on the floor, then proceeded to lay out flatbread, jam, and cubes of feta cheese before us.

"They have invited us to eat with them," Glenn said.

I nodded politely and waited for them to start eating. As we all sat around enjoying the food, Glenn kept talking. I could tell from Glenn's excitement that the conversation must have been going well. I was eager to know what they were saying, but I knew I would have to wait until the men left.

Finally, at about three o'clock, everyone decided it was time to go. Our friends gave their visitors the traditional embrace and three kisses on the cheek. After their visitors left, the four men from the bus also had to leave so they could catch another bus.

Glenn and I were soon alone in the room.

"So what did you talk about?" I asked, anxious to hear it all.

Glenn stood up and stretched. "It was so interesting, eh? They told me that most of the Turkmen live in the northeastern part of Iran."

"Around where Raheem lives at Gonbad-e-Kavus?"* I asked.

"Yeah," Glenn replied. "If we want to get to know some Turkmen, it looks like the place to be."

I could hardly believe it. The location was perfect. Raheem lived right in the middle of the greatest concentration of Turkmen in all of Iran. While visiting him, hopefully we would also be able to make contact with other Turkmen in the area.

Glenn and I planned to be in Iran for eleven days, so we decided to head four hundred miles west to Tehran before making our way to Gonbad-e-Kavus. In Tehran we could register our presence in the country at the South African embassy. We both thought it was a prudent precaution to take before heading out among the obscure towns and villages of northeastern Iran. If something happened, at least someone would know we were in the country.

---

* pronounced goombet-e-kauwoos

By the time we had finalized our plan, it was after four o'clock, so we decided to set out for Tehran the following morning. We spent our second night in the boardinghouse, this time sharing our room with a different group of Turkmen traders who had come in for the night.

Early the next morning I set off in search of transportation. Our friends from the bus had advised us the best way to get from Mashad to Tehran was by train, so I headed for the train station. When I arrived at the station, it was packed with people waiting for the trains. Asking in Farsi, I got directions to the line where tickets to Tehran were sold. Unfortunately, about two hundred people were ahead of me, and the line seemed to be moving at a snail's pace. I estimated it would take four or five hours to reach the ticket booth at the front of the line. Unwilling to wait that long, I walked to the front of the line where a soldier sat at a small table. I asked him if there was an alternative way to buy a train ticket.

"Sit there," the soldier said, pointing to a spot between him and the ticket booth.

Having nothing to lose, I sat down as instructed and waited to see what would happen next.

When the man at the booth had finished purchasing his ticket, the soldier beckoned for me to step up to the booth. As I stood up I glanced back at the long line behind me and felt a little guilty. I gave an apologetic smile in the hopes it would ease any frustrated feelings people may have had at my jumping to the head of the line, even if it had not been deliberate on my part. The man in the ticket booth understood my Farsi well, but he was unsure if there were any tickets to Tehran left for that day. Perhaps it was due to the glum look on my face at the news, but in the end he produced two second-class tickets for the 5:30 P.M. train.

"How long is the train ride?" I asked as I pulled the correct amount of rial out of my wallet.

"Around fourteen hours," the ticket seller replied.

At 5:15 that evening, Glenn and I arrived back at the train station, tickets in hand and ready to begin the long trip to Tehran. Within minutes a diesel locomotive grunted to a halt at the platform, and a flood of passengers disembarked from its overcrowded carriages. Once the crowd had dissipated, Glenn and I jostled our way aboard the train, along with several hundred other people.

We found our way to the compartment that matched the number on our ticket and opened the door. It was a six-seater compartment, and four people were already there.

I nodded a polite greeting to our fellow passengers and took a quick look around at them without trying to appear as if I were staring. Two Iranian women sat together wearing black *chadors* from head to toe with heavy veils over their faces. The other two passengers were men.

As I stowed my bag on the overhead luggage rack, I noticed that our arrival in the compartment seemed to create a problem for the other passengers. They whispered among themselves and raised their eyebrows. And then, as Glenn and I sat down, all four of them stood up and left the compartment. Several minutes later the two men returned and took their seats. We never saw the two women again.

Just before the train jerked away from the station, two more men joined us in the compartment, filling it to capacity. We had just enough room to all sit shoulder to shoulder, three on each side, with no room whatsoever to stretch out. I wondered how we were going to get any sleep that night.

The train was only a few minutes behind schedule when it pulled out of the station. Within minutes we had left Mashad behind and were rumbling along through the Iranian countryside on our way to Tehran.

As the *clickety-clack* of the train wheels settled into a monotonous rhythm, I sat thinking about how much more pleasant it was riding on the train. Unlike the bus, the train didn't have to stop at checkpoints every few miles. But no sooner had I thought this than the train pulled into a station and a police officer cradling an automatic rifle appeared at the door of our compartment.

"Prayer time," he announced with a scowl on his face.

Muslims are required to pray five times each day at specified times, even if they happen to be traveling by train. Immediately our four companions jumped to their feet and filed out into the crowded passageway. Glenn and I did not make a move, though, and the police officer ignored us and shut the door.

The two of us watched out the window as the other passengers on the train got off and made their way into two separate prayer halls located beside the station. One hall was for men and the other for women. Even though we could not see inside, I had witnessed enough Muslim prayer times in my travels to know what was happening. Everyone would be kneeling on thin mats while a mullah chanted prayers in Arabic. It didn't seem to matter that few Iranians knew Arabic.

"What happens if a local person says he doesn't want to go?" Glenn asked.

"See the guard with the notebook?" I said.

Glenn nodded his head.

"He writes down the names of anyone who won't pray. They'll end up in some sort of official trouble."

After twenty minutes the prayer time was over, and people made their way back to the train. Once all the passengers were safely aboard, the train rumbled off again. Everyone in the compartment sat in silence for an hour or so. Finally one of the men spoke. "It is time to sleep," he announced.

I watched carefully to see how this feat was going to be accomplished. First the four Iranian men stood up and moved into the small alcove by the door. Glenn and I followed their lead. Once we were all packed into the alcove, the oldest man in the group folded out the seats we had been sitting on, until they met in the middle. The compartment had been transformed into a large bed.

However, I could foresee one huge problem with the arrangement. It was impossible for six grown men to all fit on the bed together. Evidently, though, we were supposed to try. The man who pulled out the seats smiled at us all, crawled to the far side of the bed, and lay down. Without needing to be told, a second man crawled across and lay down next to him, but with his head beside the other man's feet. The other two men followed, until only Glenn and I were left standing in the alcove.

Glenn looked at me and then at the tiny space on the edge of the bed. There was just enough room for him to lie down sideways. He maneuvered himself into position, but now there was no room for me to lie down. I looked around and wondered what to do. Directly above my head was a metal luggage rack. I reached up and pulled down the bag that was on it, stuffing it in the corner of the alcove. I then pulled myself up and managed to wriggle my body into place on the rack. As soon as I had done so, I knew I had made a big mistake. Only about a four-inch clearance remained between the ceiling and me. There was no possibility of changing position and certainly not rolling over while I slept.

I lay on my back on the luggage rack for an hour, my belt digging into my back, and my left foot itching. Every time I felt the train curve left, I braced myself so I did not roll off and tumble down on the others. When I finally maneuvered myself to glance down at Glenn, he looked no more comfortable than I. "How's it going?" I whispered.

"Rotten, eh?" Glenn said. "Are you comfortable up there?"

"Not really," I said. "Do you want to swap places for a while? You're shorter than I am and might find it more comfortable up here."

Glenn nodded his head, and I wiggled my way to the edge of the luggage rack and lowered myself to the floor.

"Most coffins have more headroom," Glenn commented dryly as he maneuvered himself into position and I tried to devise a way to cling to the edge of the bed.

We both tried to lie still, but every so often Glenn would make a comment about how uncomfortable he was. I knew neither of us would get any sleep until the next prayer time.

Sure enough, at 4:30 A.M. the train lurched to a halt, and once again a policeman appeared outside the door to our compartment. Silently our traveling companions got up from the bed and walked out to join the stream of sleepy passengers making their way to the prayer hall beside the station.

"This is better," I said, grinning at Glenn as I stretched out on the bed. "Come on down. At least we'll get a good nap."

For the next half hour, Glenn and I had the luxury of stretching out on the makeshift bed. However, when our four fellow passengers returned from the mandatory prayer time, it signaled the end of night. The bed was transformed back into the hard, straight-backed seats, and once again we found ourselves sitting shoulder to shoulder staring across at one another.

By now the whole train was awake. I could hear a couple in the next compartment laughing, and a baby in a compartment farther down the car was screaming.

At 8 A.M. on the dot, the train pulled into the central station in Tehran. Glenn and I had already decided that the first item of business we would take care of was to register our presence in Iran. We could have gone to the Swiss embassy, but Glenn was eager to go to the South African embassy. I didn't care one way or the other, just as long as someone in an official capacity knew we were here in case we ran into any difficulties. After the four men had left, we pulled our bags down from the luggage rack, stepped out into the corridor, and were swept along by the crowd down the stairs and onto the station platform. It was much like any other busy terminal, except all the women were dressed exactly alike in long black robes from head to foot, and most of the men wore black, too. Glenn and I fought our way through the crowd to the curb, where we hailed a cab. We were eager to register our presence and get on with our trip.

FIVE

Links in a Chain

THE South African embassy, a white gothic-style building with two fluted columns in front, rose before us. Glenn and I made our way up the stairs that surrounded the building and entered by a side entrance. Inside the door a woman sat behind a glass partition. Glenn told her he wanted to register his presence in Iran, and she smiled and directed him to a counter on the far side of the lobby.

The polished marble floor of the embassy squeaked beneath my shoes as we strolled across it. A cluster of brown leather couches adorned the center of the lobby. Glenn stopped beside the coffee table in front of one of the couches and thumbed through the pile of South African magazines and newspapers arranged on it.

Glenn told the clerk who sat behind the counter what we wanted, and the man slid a large black journal across the counter to us. "Write your names and travel information here," he said in even more heavily accented English than Glenn's.

I jotted my name and address down in the book after Glenn, though I doubted it would do me any good if we got into trouble, since I was a Swiss citizen. Still, registering our names seemed to make Glenn more relaxed, and I felt a certain comfort and security myself knowing that at least one foreign embassy knew I was in the country.

When we had finished writing all the pertinent information, the clerk read our entries. "There are no restrictions on travel for foreigners at present," he told us. "You can travel where you like. But just in case there's a problem, let me see your travel documents."

We both handed over our passports and visas, and the clerk thumbed through them. "Everything seems to be in order," he said, handing them back to us.

A Western order of décor filled the embassy's large lobby, inviting people to enjoy the pleasant ambiance. Glenn and I decided to sit down for a while on one of the brown leather couches and enjoy some foreign newspapers. Within five minutes, another man sat down beside us. He was obviously Iranian and eager to strike up a conversation.

"Are you South African?" he asked us both.

"I am," Glenn replied.

"Really?" he said. "I am very interested in going to your country."

I listened quietly as the two of them talked about what South Africa was like. The young man soon told us his name was Mohammed and that he was a hydro engineer. Glenn had studied and worked in that same field before moving to Turkmenistan, and his eyes lit up with interest. Soon the two of them were deep in conversation. I began to wonder if this was another special meeting God had arranged for us. My impression was confirmed when Glenn told Mohammed we were interested in traveling to many different parts of Iran.

"Well, you must come and stay with me!" he exclaimed. "I am staying here for the day to see about my visa, and then I will be heading back home to Isfahan." Turning to me he added, "You really must come and visit!"

Glenn and I looked at each other, and he nodded gently. "Thank you," I said to Mohammed. "We would like that."

Mohammed handed us a business card and then proceeded to tell us a little about Isfahan, a city of about two million people, 180 miles south of Tehran.

After we had talked for a few minutes, Mohammed was called into one of the embassy offices, and Glenn and I decided it was time to be on our way. We shook hands, thanking him for his kind invitation, and promised we would meet again within the next couple of days.

"How about that, eh?" Glenn said as we emerged into the bright winter sunlight of Tehran.

"It's pretty amazing. How many hydro engineers would you expect to run into in a city as large as Tehran? It sounds to me like an open invitation to visit Isfahan," I said. "It looks like our prayers are being answered."

"When do you think we should go?" Glenn asked.

As we walked along the busy streets, we decided to spend the rest of the day in Tehran and head for Isfahan early the next morning. Our plan was to stay with Mohammed for a few days and then make our way north to visit Raheem in Gonbad-e-Kavus, where most of the Turkmen lived.

The following morning we arrived at the bus station bright and early. It was a crisp winter day, and the snow-capped peaks of the Elburz Mountains towered majestically over the city as we rumbled out of Tehran and into the Iranian countryside. It was so much more relaxing than our previous bus trip to Mashad. Now we were traveling inside Iran, and the nerve-wracking business of crossing the border with all of the searches and suspicious guards was behind us.

As the bus headed south, I couldn't help thinking of how inexpensive it was to travel here. In terms of the one American dollar the fare had cost each of us, the trip was a great bargain, but not in terms of the length of time it took to travel 180 miles. The trip took eight hours, and we arrived in Isfahan at about four o'clock in the afternoon.

The city of Isfahan was even more beautiful than Mohammed had described it. The Zayandeh River ran through the center of the city, and Glenn and I stopped to marvel at an ancient bridge that spanned its breadth.

From the bus station we headed down the street in search of a cheap hotel. We only had to walk a mile before we found one that fit our budget of five dollars each a night.

Once we were safely in our hotel room, we called Mohammed to see if he had made it back from Tehran yet. The phone rang twice before someone answered it.

"Hello, Mohammed?" Glenn asked.

As I listened quietly to one side of the conversation, it sounded as though Mohammed was still eager to be our host.

Glenn was smiling when he finally put down the phone. "He insists we don't spend the night here," he said, relaying the conversation to me. "He insists that we are to be his guests the whole time we are in Isfahan. He'll be by in ten minutes to pick us up and take us to dinner."

"Wow," I replied, "that's really nice of him."

"It sure is. I wonder what God is up to, eh?" Glenn nodded. "Anyway, we need to get our bags and meet Mohammed out front. He'll be driving a light blue Fiat."

Sure enough, ten minutes later a light blue Fiat pulled up in front of the hotel, and Mohammed jumped out to greet us warmly.

"How about a hamburger?" he asked as we loaded our bags into the trunk.

"Sounds great to me," I responded, always ready to fill up on junk food.

Mohammed took us to a restaurant not too far from the hotel, and we sat at a bar and ordered hamburgers and milkshakes. I was surprised at how crowded the place was. A number of college students were sitting or standing in small groups while munching burgers and fries, just like I was used to seeing in an American city.

After a few minutes of small talk, our conversation with Mohammed turned serious. He wanted to know all about why we had come to Iran, why we followed Jesus, and how Christianity differed from the Muslim religion he had been raised in.

As we talked and shared our faith, he listened carefully, nodding and asking questions every few minutes. When Glenn was talking, I prayed silently for Mohammed, asking God to open his mind and give him understanding of the Good News. I knew Glenn was doing the same while I talked.

After the meal, we piled back into the little Fiat and headed south. Fifteen minutes later we pulled up in front of a large apartment complex. Mohammed looked around nervously as he got out of the car. Following his lead, I looked around, too, wondering what we were looking for.

"Secret police," Mohammed whispered. "I think it's some kind of offense to have a foreigner stay at your house without all the proper paperwork."

My stomach suddenly knotted up, and I kept watching the shadows around the edges of the buildings as we walked quickly to the nearest door and climbed the stairs to the fourth floor.

"I'm taking you to my friend Nasir's house," Mohammed said as we walked down a long, dimly lit corridor. "He's a fourth-year political science major, and he lives alone at the moment. I thought it would be better if we all stayed with him."

When we finally reached the door of his friend's apartment, Mohammed knocked faintly. Almost immediately the door swung open, and a stocky young man stood in the doorway smiling at us. He put out his hand and said, "Welcome, I'm Nasir. Please come on in."

As we walked into a large living room, I noticed there was no Western-style furniture in sight, just a pile of carpets, pillows, and a few folded blankets. We dropped our bags in the corner and sat cross-legged on the floor as Mohammed made introductions. Soon we were drinking tea with our new friends and engaged in a lively conversation on a variety of interests.

It was three o'clock in the morning before we finished talking about all the changes in Iran and how different life was in the West. Neither Mohammed nor Nasir had any idea about what it was like to live in a Western country.

Glenn and I went to bed very happy that night. We had so much to be grateful for. It seemed at every juncture of our trip, God was blessing us and leading us to the right people. The following morning we ate breakfast at a nearby restaurant and then spent several hours walking around Isfahan, enjoying all the beautiful sights and its ancient carpet bazaar.

We arrived back at the apartment at around three in the afternoon. Nasir was already back from his day at college and was eager to talk with us again about spiritual matters. Around seven o'clock, Mohammed arrived and eagerly joined in the discussion. Together we talked for another hour before we decided to go out for dinner.

This time we ate Iranian food at a local restaurant, and then Mohammed took us on a tour of the city. Isfahan was stunning at night. So many people were strolling around, or talking and drinking in the many small cafés that lined the city's streets. We stopped to buy an ice cream and strolled over one of the bridges that crossed the Zayandeh River. As we walked, Mohammed filled us in on some of the more interesting points of the city's history. He told us Isfahan had once been the capital of Iran, and that it was famous for its traditionally manufactured tiles, rugs, and cotton fabrics.

Glenn and I had decided we should travel back to Tehran the next day before going on to Gonbad-e-Kavus, so we told Mohammed of our plans.

"How are you going to get there?" he asked.

I shrugged. "By bus, I guess, the same way we came."

"You should try flying like I did," he replied. "It's one of the cheapest ways to get around in Iran."

"Really?" I questioned, not quite believing him. "How much would it cost to fly to Tehran?"

"About ten dollars," he replied.

"Ten dollars!" I repeated. "That's amazing. I had no idea it was so cheap."

"That's because the airline is very heavily subsidized by the government. I can take you to a travel agency that is open late if you like," Mohammed said.

Half an hour later Glenn and I had airline tickets to Tehran, departing at 11:45 P.M. on December 31. We would be flying as the Western calendar changed to 1997. Just as Mohammed had predicted, the tickets cost us ten dollars per person.

The following morning, New Year's Eve, I awoke before Glenn and decided to sit outside in the early morning sun and read my Bible and pray for the next part of our trip. As I prayed, I experienced something unusual. The words "You are going to have to go to the bottom before you get out of here" popped into my head and began repeating themselves. I opened my eyes and pondered the statement. What did it mean? And what was the bottom, anyway? I wanted to dismiss the words as just my wild imagination, but somehow I couldn't get them out of my mind or the thought that God might be saying something to me through them. If this was a message for me, though, I wasn't quite sure what it was. I tried to think of what the "bottom" might refer to, but I had no idea. It never crossed my mind that God was gently preparing me for the worst experience of my life.

Later that evening, Mohammed and Nasir escorted us to Isfahan's airport. Along the way the two of them asked us more questions about Jesus and what He meant in our lives. We were more than glad to answer their questions and tell them what He could do for them. When we got to the airport, it was hard to say good-bye. Our two new friends had let us share their lives for two days, and we had learned a lot about them, their faith, and their country.

The flight back to Tehran was full. In just the few days I had been in Iran, I was beginning to conclude that every form of transport was always crowded. During the flight, the words from my prayer time, "You are going to go to the bottom," echoed over and over in my head, but I did not share that with Glenn. There was no need for both of us to be confused by whatever it meant.

After we landed in Tehran, we took a cab back to the same guesthouse where we had stayed before and turned in for a few hours sleep before morning.

When we finally got up, we decided to travel on to Gonbad-e-Kavus, though we had a frustrating time trying to find the exact spot where the bus departed from. The whole bus departure system seemed to be very arbitrary. Fortunately, Glenn noticed a Mercedes minibus with a Gonbad-e-Kavus sign hanging in the front window, and we quickly climbed aboard for the next leg of our journey.

Compared to the first bus ride we had experienced, this one was delightful and relaxing. After several hours of driving, the Caspian Sea came into view, and we began to drive through small beachside communities. It made me feel nostalgic for the beachside communities of California where I had grown up.

At about six o'clock in the evening, the minibus pulled into the town of Gonbad-e-Kavus. As we clambered off the bus, we thanked the driver. We showed Raheem's address to several local people standing around, and the consensus seemed to be that the street Raheem's house was located on was to the south. We began walking, and every block or so we asked someone else if we were still headed in the right direction. Finally, a man on a bike pointed to a large house with an iron gate.

"There," he said. "That's where you want to go."

We opened the wrought-iron gate and walked across the courtyard to the front door. I took a deep breath before knocking. We waited a minute or two, and then a young man about twenty-five years old appeared at the door. I told him who we were, and he introduced himself as Ahmed, Raheem's oldest son. Ahmed invited us to come in and sit in the living room while he went to get his father.

Glenn and I sat down on some pillows to wait for our host to appear. Several exquisite handmade Persian rugs covered the floor.

Soon Raheem appeared at the door. His face lit up as he entered the room, and I could see he was genuinely pleased to see us. I introduced him to Glenn, and we were soon in the middle of an animated three-way conversation. Glenn spoke to Raheem and his son in Turkmen, and I spoke to them in Farsi, while Glenn and I spoke to each other in English. It all seemed to work out surprisingly well, for we had no problem in communicating.

By now it was dinnertime, and Raheem showed us into an adjoining room, where we washed our hands in a bowl. Just as we were drying our hands, someone knocked at the door. Ahmed went to answer it and stooped down to pick up the trays of food that had been left on the floor just outside. He brought the trays into the room and set them on a tablecloth that had been spread out on the floor. I knew that the women in the house had prepared the food and left it outside so that they would not have to have any contact with the males of the household or their guests. During my years in Muslim countries, I had become used to this strict cultural differentiation between men and women, even within the privacy of a person's own home.

The women had prepared for us one of the best meals I had eaten in a long time. It consisted of a wonderful spicy fish dish, along with rice and Iranian flatbread.

As we ate, Raheem asked us what our plans were. I explained we were planning to stay in a local hotel, but he immediately insisted we stay in his house for the whole time we would be there.

During the next few days, Raheem proceeded to show us Iranian hospitality at its best. We visited the new bread distribution shop where one of his younger sons worked. Raheem also showed us the bread factory where he worked. Ahmed even took us to a horse track to see a demonstration of the famed Turkmen horsemanship. Then, best of all, we were driven out into the countryside in search of a traditional Turkmen settlement. The place we went to was nothing more than a grouping of large felt tents, which the nomadic Turkmen people took with them as they followed their sheep to summer and winter pastures. I knew that these traditional settlements were now rare, as the Soviets had tried to break down the Turkmen way of life and resettle the people into low-cost apartments.

During our stay in Gonbad-e-Kavus, we also went in search of Mustafa's second cousin so we could deliver in person the letter he had given us back in Turkmenistan.

When we finally arrived at the address on the envelope, we were immediately welcomed inside the house and treated as if we were old friends. The family read the letter we had for them and pored over some photos of Mustafa and his family that were also enclosed in the envelope. Then, like visits in so many other countries, the photo albums came out, and Glenn and I were given the rundown on the entire clan.

Tea and sweets were served while we talked, and by the time we left, we felt we had made new friends. Glenn and I were excited by the visit. God was indeed guiding us, and our tennis court plans were coming true. We had come to Iran hoping we could be a link in the chain that would soon unite Turkmen Christians in Turkmenistan with their distant relatives in Iran.

When we got back to Raheem's house that day, he was just arriving home from work. We fell into a lengthy conversation. At one point he turned to me and asked in Farsi, "Have you gotten a registration stamp in your passport since you arrived?"

"No," I replied, my heart rate quickening slightly. Anything to do with borders and official papers made me a little nervous.

"Then don't worry. It will be okay," Raheem said.

"Okay," I replied. "But let me know if there is anything Glenn and I should be doing about it."

Raheem nodded.

I took the nod to mean Raheem would investigate further to see if we needed this particular stamp and get back to us if we did. However, he never mentioned the matter again, and I didn't think any more about it. After all, I told myself, no one at the South African embassy had mentioned that we needed a registration stamp. If it were that important, surely they would have told us.

SIX

An Unexpected Detour

IT was eight o'clock in the morning, January 6, 1997, and Glenn and I were eating our last breakfast in Iran. Raheem sat to my left, and Ahmed, his oldest son, to my right.

"I have some news for you," Raheem said as we ate. "I must go out of town today, so I have asked Ahmed to escort you to the border. I apologize for not being able to go with you myself."

"That's okay. Everything should be fine," I replied, picking another flatbread from the basket in front of me. But as I spoke, deep down I was disappointed Raheem would not be accompanying us. As a cleric, he was a well-respected member of the community, and wherever we went with him, everyone we came in contact with treated us as honored guests. While Ahmed had the same family name, he was only twenty-five years old and didn't seem to command the same level of respect as his father.

Still, I reasoned, what could go wrong without Raheem along? Our paperwork was all in order, I still had the slip of paper recording the amount of money I'd brought into the country, and we were leaving Iran well within the allotted time stipulated by our visas. I told myself everything would be fine, and by this time tomorrow we would be safely back in Ashgabad.

After breakfast I rolled up the new rug I'd purchased and stuffed it into the extra bag I had bought at the local market the day before. I packed the rest of my belongings into my maroon leather bag. Soon Glenn and I were both ready for the trip back to Ashgabad.

We thanked Raheem for his great hospitality and then set out with Ahmed to catch a bus to Ashgabad via Inc-e Born, a border crossing about fifty miles north of Gonbad-e-Kavus. The trip to Inc-e Born took about two hours, and we arrived at the remote crossing a little before midday.

This border crossing was very different from the one we had crossed on our way to Mashad. That one was equipped to handle multiple busloads of people entering the country. This crossing, however, was not only smaller and more remote, but it seemed the main traffic flow here was huge oil tankers. Across the border was the town of Gudryolum, Turkmenistan.

The bus stopped in front of a small stone customs building located beside the border crossing. Glenn and I, accompanied by Ahmed, took our bags and made our way inside. My heart dropped when I saw four long lines of people waiting to be processed through customs. We looked at each other and then picked a line to join. It took us about thirty minutes to get to the front.

When our turn came, we placed our bags on the table in front of the customs officer and answered the usual questions: How long have you been in the country? Did you buy anything while you were here? Have you had any problems of an official nature?

The officer seemed satisfied with our answers and turned his attention to our bags. He unzipped my leather bag first, turning it upside down and emptying all of its contents onto the table. Something told me we were in for a thorough search. The customs officer patted down the bag, checking for secret compartments, and then began a meticulous examination of each item on the table. The first thing he picked up was a shirt. He checked the pockets and felt the collar for lumps before placing it on the left side of the table. Next he picked up my camera. I watched with a straight face as he flicked it open and pulled out the film and batteries. Without changing the intense look of concentration on his face, the officer placed the film and batteries to the right, and my disabled camera to the left on top of the shirt.

I continued to watch silently as the officer meticulously divided everything that had been in my bag into two piles at either end of the table. I soon realized that these two piles represented the belongings I would be allowed to keep and those that were going to be confiscated. While I was annoyed by the man's brazen actions, I knew it was useless to try to say anything or show any emotion on my face. Past experience had taught me that in this part of the world customs officers thoroughly enjoyed the amount of power they exercised and did not respond well to being challenged.

As the customs officer continued to sort through my belongings, I glanced at Glenn. His face was white with shock at what was happening.

When the officer was finished with my personal effects, he unzipped Glenn's bag and dumped its contents onto the table. He then repeated the same process, dividing Glenn's belongings into two piles.

As I watched the official at work, something didn't quite add up. I knew it was his job to search our bags, which he was doing very thoroughly, but somehow it seemed more of a charade than a deliberate act. I began to wonder where the search might lead. Was the customs officer just trying to gather a few Western "souvenirs" from us, or was there something more sinister going on behind the scene?

"Put your things back in your bags and step over to immigration control," the officer finally instructed.

Relief welled up inside me. The customs check was over. Now it was just immigration to clear, and we would be back on the bus and on our way across the border to Turkmenistan.

Glenn and I stuffed our possessions back into our bags while the customs officer found a cardboard box and packed the items he had confiscated from us into it.

It was only fifteen feet from the customs check to immigration, and I was eager to get my passport stamped and be on my way. As I waited for an immigration officer to arrive, I tried not to nervously bite my fingernails. It was a struggle.

Finally, an immigration officer appeared, but he did not ask to see any of our passports. Instead, he nodded at us and said, "Please take a seat and wait."

Glenn and I did as instructed, but by then I was starting to get concerned. An hour went by and the immigration officer had not reappeared, though there seemed to be a lot of activity going on in the small office behind the counter.

Shortly thereafter, the officer poked his head out and motioned for Ahmed to come into the back office. When he had disappeared, Glenn turned to me and asked, "I wonder what that's all about?"

"I wish I knew," I whispered back. "This is all getting a little weird."

Ten minutes passed before Ahmed reappeared. "They need to see your passports," he said.

I stood up, ready to walk into the office he had just come out of and try to talk to the official.

"No, no. You don't understand," Ahmed said. "They want me to take your passports into them. They do not want to see you."

Ahmed must have noticed the worried look on my face, because he added, "Not right now, anyway. In a few minutes they will call you."

Reluctantly Glenn and I handed over our passports. Despite Ahmed's reassurances that everything would be fine, we both had an uneasy feeling.

"Raheem's family has a lot of respect in this area," I said, breaking the silence.

Glenn nodded glumly. "Let's hope so."

By now it was midafternoon, and most of our fellow passengers had been processed through customs and immigration and were back on the bus. I knew the bus driver would not wait indefinitely for Glenn and me. In an attempt to divert my mind from worrying about what would happen if the bus left without us, I watched several oil tankers pull up to the checkpoint. My eyes followed one driver as he entered the building and proceeded through customs and immigration. He was back in his truck in less than five minutes. I envied him. Why was it taking us so long to get out of Iran?

Half an hour after taking our passports into the office, Ahmed reappeared.

"Where are our passports?" I asked as calmly as possible when I realized he was empty-handed.

Ahmed smiled nervously. "They'll call you in to get them in a minute," he said. "There are a couple of things they want to check," he said nervously.

"What things?" I asked.

"I'm not sure," Ahmed replied. "But they said it won't take long."

In fact, it did take a long time. An hour later we were still waiting to be called. Finally, the immigration official called Ahmed back into the office again. This time we could hear voices rising and falling in heated argument. It was too far away to understand what they were saying, but Ahmed was arguing fervently about something.

When Ahmed came back, the expression on his face was flat with defeat. He threw his hands into the air in frustration. "We still have to wait," he said.

"Is there a problem?" I asked.

"Yes," he said with a certain finality in his voice.

"What's the problem?" I asked.

"Well, just wait," Ahmed replied. "Hopefully it will be okay. I have to go back in and talk some more."

This time when Ahmed left, Glenn and I prayed for the situation. But as we prayed, I had a difficult time trying not to think the worst. Perhaps they knew I was an American and had decided to detain me as a result. Then again, maybe they would just stamp my passport *persona non grata* so I would never be welcome back in the country. I didn't know what to expect, and the apprehension of not knowing was starting to give me stomach cramps. I finally gave in and began biting my nails anxiously as I waited.

The hands on my watch seemed to move at a snail's pace, but finally Ahmed emerged from the office again. He was empty-handed and frustrated. The crestfallen look on his face did nothing to calm me. He grabbed the handle of one of my bags.

"Let's go," he said, jerking it off the floor.

"What do you mean, 'Let's go'?" I asked, my heart pounding.

"Take your things. We have to go back into town," Ahmed said.

"But what about our passports?" I questioned.

Ahmed paused for a moment. "They have taken them."

"What do you mean they've taken them!" I could hear the panic rising in my voice. "Where have they taken them?"

Ahmed shrugged. "I am sorry. I don't know much, but they've confiscated them," he said.

"Isn't there someone we can talk to?" I asked, convinced Ahmed had given in too easily. I reminded myself he was a local and probably unaware that foreigners could be jailed in Iran for not having their passport on them at all times. It was inconceivable to me that an immigration officer, who obviously knew this, would send us away without our passports.

Ahmed put my bag down and sighed. "I will see what I can do."

This time it was only a matter of a minute or two before he beckoned us to follow him into the back office.

"We need our passports," I said in Farsi, looking the immigration official squarely in the eye.

"I am sure your friend has told you that will not be possible. We have found some irregularities in them," he said.

I opened my mouth to speak again, but he held up his hand to stop me. "Here is the address where you can pick up your passports in a few days," he said, folding the notepaper he had written the address on four times and handing it to me. "It is a small matter. Now if you will excuse me," he said, pointing toward the door. The tone of his voice and the look he gave me made it clear that the issue was closed.

I walked out, my mind spinning. Something was seriously wrong with the way events were playing themselves out. *Why, God, when we are right at the border?* I thought as we stood outside the office, wondering what to do next.

"Let's get out of here," Glenn said. "How about we get something to eat out of their earshot?"

I nodded. We needed time to think and consider our options, which seemed very limited at that point.

Outside the building was a small kiosk with two tables and some chairs beside it. We ordered some rice and kabobs and sat down. While we were waiting for our food, the bus driver came over and talked to Ahmed. He smiled weakly at Glenn and me before heading back to the bus. Moments later, in a billow of black diesel fumes, the bus headed off for Ashgabad without us.

My heart sank as I watched the bus cross the border and then unfolded the slip of paper the immigration officer had given to me. I could scarcely believe what I read. The address on the paper was back in Tehran. Tehran! It would take more than ten hours traveling to return there.

"You're not going to believe this," I said, turning to look at Glenn. "We're supposed to return to Tehran to get our passports."

I watched Glenn's face turn pale. "How can we do that?" he questioned. "We're not supposed to go outside the house without our passports. We could end up in serious trouble trying to go to Tehran without them."

For a second I was amused by the irony of Glenn's statement. It was obvious we were already in serious trouble!

"What were you arguing about in the office?" I asked Ahmed.

"The registration stamp. Neither of you has a registration stamp in your passport."

I thought for a moment. "Your father asked us if we had one, and when I told him we didn't, he said it would be okay. I thought that meant it wasn't a big deal. And what difference does it make now? We were on our way out of the country."

Ahmed said nothing in reply. He just shrugged his shoulders sheepishly.

"They can't be serious about us going all the way back to Tehran to get our passports," I said, venting my pent-up frustrations. "That's asking us to break the law. For us to travel without a passport is one hundred percent illegal. I'm going back in there to tell them so!" I announced, my American sense of justice rising within me.

"No, no, my friend," Ahmed said, putting his hand on my arm. "Let me go back and explain the situation to them again. Maybe they will listen to me this time."

Glenn and I said little to each other while Ahmed went back inside the building. I could only assume that Glenn's mind was in the same turmoil as mine.

Ten minutes later Ahmed returned and pulled up a chair beside us. "There is no choice," he said. "I am terribly sorry, but it appears we must do what they say." He appeared to be on the verge of tears, and as precarious as our situation was, I found myself feeling compassion for him. His father had sent him to escort us, the family's honored guests, across the border, and he had failed in his efforts.

"We'll find a way through this," I heard myself say to Ahmed. "Don't worry. It will work out okay."

By now it was late in the afternoon, and there seemed little else to do but return to Gonbad-e-Kavus and regroup at Raheem's house.

For the return trip, Ahmed arranged for us to ride in a pickup truck. As we slung our bags in the back of the truck, I offered to sit back there for the trip, since there was not enough room in the cab for us all. I wanted to be alone with my thoughts, which by then had turned grim and dark. I needed to think and pray. I didn't know what lay ahead for Glenn and me, but it was beginning to look ominous.

The pickup truck dropped us off at Raheem's gate. Raheem was not in when we got back, but he was certainly surprised to see us when he arrived home late in the evening.

Ahmed carefully explained the situation to his father, who asked many questions, most of which had no sensible answer. "I cannot understand it," Raheem said several times, shaking his head. "There was no need to take your passports."

"What should we do now?" I asked.

"Tomorrow I will take you to the local immigration office. Your passports would have to pass through there on their way back to Tehran. Hopefully we will be able to intercept them before they go any farther and correct this mistake."

By now my nerves were taut and on edge, and I lay awake most of the night worrying about what was going to happen in the morning. All the while Glenn snored loudly beside me. I envied his ability to shut things out and sleep so peacefully.

As the night wore on, I began to think about freedom. For me freedom was having a passport and being able to go where I pleased. As an American, it was something that I felt I was entitled to. It was my right. Then it hit me. When I gave my life over to Jesus, I also gave over the right to run my life the way I saw fit. As the apostle Paul put it, I was no longer my own. I had been bought with a price. Of course I had heard those words a thousand times, but now, stranded in Iran without my passport and my freedom, I was gaining a deeper appreciation of what it meant to take the backseat and allow God to take complete control of my life.

However, doubt crept in along with that revelation. I had been in my share of jams at various borders around the world and always managed to get through, so why had this border crossing turned out so different? I believed God was going to "come through" for me in this situation, but somewhere deep inside lurked the feeling that this matter was a long way from over.

At breakfast the next morning even Raheem looked pale and worried. While we ate, he kept patting me on the hand and telling me not to worry. "We will intercept your passports today," he kept saying.

Glenn and I, accompanied by Raheem, arrived at the immigration office at ten o'clock. The office was a small, dimly lit building in the heart of Gonbad-e-Kavus. As we climbed the stairs that led to the front door, Raheem lowered his voice and cautioned us to let him do all the talking.

"Don't speak unless you are asked a direct question," he advised us. "It will be easier for you that way."

Glenn and I both nodded, eager to do whatever Raheem felt was necessary to get the situation resolved. All we wanted to do was get our passports back, catch a bus, and cross over to the safety of Turkmenistan.

As soon as we stepped inside, we were ushered into a private office where a high-ranking official greeted us.

Raheem told the official how we'd had our passports confiscated at the border for no apparent reason and explained that we needed them back immediately so that we could return to Turkmenistan. He also went into great detail explaining that we could not travel to Tehran to get them because, as the official well knew, it was illegal for any foreigner to travel anywhere without a passport on his or her person.

I watched the official intently as the conversation progressed. He nodded his head at the appropriate moments, but he seemed mildly bored by the whole affair.

Finally, Raheem asked the official directly to hand our passports back.

The immigration officer sprang to life and produced our passports from a large envelope lying on top of his desk. "Unfortunately, I cannot return these to you," he said. "As you can see, they do not have the required registration stamps in them."

"What does it matter now, my friend?" Raheem asked. "Surely you can stamp them and allow my guests to be on their way out of Iran."

The official shook his head. "There are certain rules," he said in a resigned voice. "And rules have to be followed."

His words jarred me. Yes, the Iranians I had met had a healthy respect for rules, but something odd struck me about his statement. It seemed to me that officials could and did change the rules all the time when it suited them. Surely we had been scared enough by now. Why not let us go and tell us never to come back? What was so important about the registration stamp in our passports?

Raheem and the immigration official continued to talk, but it was obvious their conversation was going in circles. It soon became apparent that even our host's honored standing in the community was not going to get us out of this dilemma.

"Wait a few days so your passports will have been processed in Tehran, and then take a bus there to collect them," the official finally told us as he stood and escorted us from his office.

"The official assures me the whole affair will only take half an hour at the most to clear up in Tehran, and then you will be free to cross the border and go home. Until then, of course, you will remain my guests," Raheem said once we were outside the office.

Given the unexpected turn of events, we had nothing else to do but accept Raheem's hospitality and spend several more days in his home before going all the way back to Tehran.

SEVEN

"We Know a Lot More About You Than You Think!"

R A H E E M was a perfect host throughout the four extra days we spent in his home. We enjoyed many meals with him, the other male members of his family, and numerous friends he invited to his home. Many of his friends were quick to reassure us there was nothing sinister about our passports being taken. "It's just the way the government works," they would say. "All governments have their own ways of doing things." And sometimes they would ask, "The government has been very cautious of foreigners the last few years, but you men don't have anything to hide, do you?"

Our reply was always the same: "No, we have nothing to hide from the government."

"Well, everything will go fine for you, then," they would respond.

I wished I felt as confident as they did, but the truth was that deep down inside I was worried about our situation and more than a little scared. I had traveled in Central Asia enough to know that having your passport confiscated in this manner did not portend well for what might lie ahead when we reached Tehran.

That first night I lay in bed tossing and turning, questioning what we could have done differently to avoid the situation we were now facing. On the second night, I began to entertain the idea of fleeing. I thought back to the Turkmen village we had visited several days before. Ahmed had told us it was a mere twenty-minute walk from there over the hills to Turkmenistan. I had my American passport waiting for me back in Turkmenistan, and Glenn could report his stolen. It would be so easy to just flee across the border, and very little risk would be involved. As long as we didn't try to reenter Iran, there would be few serious repercussions that I could think of.

Yet deep in my heart I had doubts about going through with that plan. "Walk through whatever God has for you here," a voice inside me urged. "You don't know what will happen, or why, but God does. Trust Him."

I wrestled sleeplessly with the issue for several hours. What was more important, my freedom or following God's path? Finally, the thought came to me, "How can you go back to America and tell people God is in control of every situation in their lives if you can't let Him be in charge of your life right now?" That thought pierced my heart with conviction. If I wasn't willing to trust God here, how could I tell others to do the same?

By early morning, I had made up my mind. In a silent prayer I told the Lord I believed He was bigger than any government on earth, even the Iranian government. He was sovereign. And although I could not see that sovereignty clearly right now and my emotions were telling me otherwise, God had led me to Iran, and I would leave in His way and in His time. Regardless of what happened, I purposed in my heart I would not be like Job. I would not second-guess God. I would entrust myself and this difficult situation into His hands.

We left Gonbad-e-Kavus by bus early in the morning on January 10. Once again Raheem sent Ahmed to accompany us.

The bus made numerous stops, and it took about sixteen hours to reach Tehran. Along the way we had two heart-stopping moments at checkpoints. To my great relief, we were not asked to produce our passports. I didn't even want to think about what further complications could develop if some angry official discovered us traveling without them.

Finally, around midnight, the bus pulled to a halt at the main bus depot in Tehran. It wasn't until we climbed off the bus that Glenn and I realized we had been so preoccupied with our situation that we had not arranged for a place to stay. But then, what options did we have? To stay in a hotel in Iran, a foreigner needed to show his or her passport at the front desk. So I turned to Ahmed and asked what we should do.

At first he just shrugged his shoulders. Evidently Ahmed hadn't thought of it either. Eventually, though, he searched through his bag and pulled out a notebook. "I'll call a friend," he said, then walked toward a public telephone.

By now the crowd of passengers who had arrived on the bus had dissipated, leaving the three of us standing in a pool of light from a streetlamp. I began to feel very conspicuous and wished Ahmed would hurry up.

Finally, he hung up the phone. "Everything is okay. We can stay with my friend," he said. "But we need to find a taxi to take us there," he added, looking down the deserted street.

Right then, out of the corner of my eye, I saw a green-clad figure marching directly toward us. My heart sank. It was an Iranian soldier.

"What are these foreigners doing here?" he demanded of Ahmed.

Ahmed politely explained that we had all just got off a bus from Gonbad-e-Kavus and were about to catch a taxi to a friend's house for the night.

The soldier grunted and turned to Glenn and me. "Show me your passports!" he barked.

"My friends don't have their passports," Ahmed replied, stepping between Glenn and me and the soldier. "Their passports were sent from Gonbad-e-Kavus to an office here in Tehran, and we have come to collect them first thing in the morning."

I watched nervously as the soldier's eyes began to bulge before he exploded in rage. "It is illegal for these foreigners to be here without passports in their possession." He prodded me with his finger and then motioned with the barrel of the automatic rifle he was carrying. "Over there. I must take you to my supervisor."

In despair, Glenn and I exchanged worried glances. Our worst nightmare was coming true.

"Let me do the talking," Ahmed whispered as we were marched away by the soldier.

Not too far from the bus depot we came to a small wooden structure by the side of the road that served as a guard post. Inside sat the soldier's supervisor, lazily smoking a cigarette. He jumped to his feet and stubbed out the cigarette when we entered.

The soldier began to tell his supervisor that he had discovered two foreigners traveling without passports. Every minute or two he would turn and yell at us and prod us with his rifle.

Soon all of them were yelling at one another. As I listened to the heated conversation, it was very disconcerting to think our fate was being decided in such a volatile atmosphere.

The arguing went on for quite some time. The soldier who had apprehended us insisted we should be thrown in jail, while Ahmed asserted we were following the exact orders of the government officials who had taken our passports back at the border.

The supervisor seemed to get more and more annoyed by the situation with each passing minute. Finally, after nearly an hour of arguing back and forth between Ahmed and the soldier, the supervisor turned to us and said, "Get out of here and don't come near this bus station without your passport again. Go! Go!"

We grabbed our bags and all but ran out of the guardhouse. Wanting to put as much distance between us and the bus station as possible, we jogged along the street until we spotted a car. All three of us flagged it down, and Ahmed asked the driver if he would take us to the address of his friend. The driver agreed, and the three of us sank into the backseat of his car. It was then that I realized I was feeling nauseous and was shaking uncontrollably.

It was nearly 2 A.M. when we reached the home of Ahmed's friend, who graciously invited us in. He gave Glenn and me some cushions to sleep on in the living room, but by then we were much too churned up inside to even try to get some sleep.

On and off throughout the night, the two of us talked quietly. We quizzed each other about what was going to happen next, though neither of us had any real idea. Like me, Glenn had the uneasy feeling we might be walking into a trap, but neither of us could see any way of avoiding it now. As we prayed together about our predicament, both of us felt strongly that we should visit the South African embassy before going to retrieve our passports at the address the immigration official at the border had given us.

The next morning, when we suggested to Ahmed that we wanted to go to the embassy, he looked relieved.

"Would it be okay if I went with you in the taxi as far as the embassy and then left you there?" he asked. "That way I could catch a bus back to Gonbad-e-Kavus today."

"That will be fine," I said. "We will get some advice from the staff at the embassy before going to pick up our passports."

"The people at the embassy will be of much more help to you than me," Ahmed pointed out, the relief obvious in his voice.

I could see he was torn between being a good host and wanting to get as far away from our situation as possible. The episode with the soldier the night before had really shaken him up. Until now, I hadn't even thought of the possible repercussions for him and his family, who had been such a help to us.

At around 10 A.M. we thanked Ahmed's friend for allowing us to stay in his home and then carried our bags outside, where Ahmed had already hailed a taxi. Twenty minutes later we pulled up in front of the South African embassy. Ahmed helped us unload our bags and then said a quick good-bye before riding off in the taxi.

As we walked up to the embassy, I noticed it didn't look as busy as the last time we had visited. Soon we discovered why. The guard at the door told us it was a scheduled day off for the staff, and the embassy was closed. For a moment Glenn and I didn't know what to do. Should we go ahead and retrieve our passports without talking to officials at the embassy?

We discussed the situation for a few minutes and decided neither of us wanted to visit any more Iranian officials without first seeking advice from the embassy. Glenn explained our predicament to the guard, and he allowed us to use the phone to call Michael, one of the embassy's consular officials.

I listened as Glenn spoke to Michael in Afrikaans. When he hung up the phone, he told me Michael was on his way to pick us up. Even though he only lived two minutes' walk from the embassy, he told Glenn we would be less conspicuous if we traveled in an embassy vehicle rather than walk to his place.

Glenn had just finished telling me this when a dark brown Range Rover pulled up beside us. We threw our bags in the back and climbed in. Michael introduced himself and drove us down the street and around a corner to his residence. I breathed a sigh of relief when the gate clanged shut behind us.

We spent a quiet day with Michael, filling him in on all that had happened at the border. The following morning Glenn and I were whisked back to the South African embassy in an official vehicle. Michael had arranged for us to meet John Morris, a senior member of the embassy staff. On our arrival we were ushered into a spacious office. John Morris shook our hands and then got right down to business. He asked us what had happened when we tried to cross the border, and we recounted the events for him.

"Have you contacted the Swiss embassy?" he asked.

"No," I replied. "We decided to go through your embassy first. Do you think I should contact them now?"

"No, no. That's probably not necessary," John Morris said. "There shouldn't be any problems. We'll take care of you. In fact, I think I'll send one of our Iranian staff members with you just to make sure everything goes well. She'll be able to translate if they interrogate you. I know you speak some Farsi, but she will make sure there is no misunderstanding in what everyone says."

I must have looked alarmed because John Morris reached out and put his hand on my arm. "There are not going to be any problems, Dan. You don't need to look so worried!"

I was still trying to brush off my worries forty-five minutes later when Glenn and I and Nadia, the Iranian worker from the South African embassy, climbed into a taxi and headed for the address on the piece of paper I had been given back at the border crossing.

The address turned out to be a large modern building in downtown Tehran. When we walked through the main door, I saw numerous foreigners milling around in its main corridor. Glenn and I took our place in line, and I started up a conversation with the two men in front of us. They were both English and were on a bike tour through the country. Their trip was taking them longer than planned, and they needed to get an extension for their visas. In front of them was a man from North Africa who had lost some vital piece of paper from his passport and needed it replaced before he could leave Tehran.

As we all waited in line, people in the room swapped information with one another about where to stay and what sights to see in Tehran. As I listened to the pleasant conversations, I began to calm down a little. Even though the last few days had been unnerving, I told myself that perhaps I had let my imagination run a little wild. After all, the room was filled with foreigners in various stages of legal limbo, so why should I think Glenn and I were special cases that had been singled out for harassment? It might take an hour or so to correct our paperwork, but no one we spoke to had been told to come back for a second day. Seeing so many other people having their issues resolved, I began to feel quite optimistic.

We had been waiting for about twenty minutes when an official made his way along the line checking everyone's paperwork. When he finally reached us, I pulled out the slip of paper I'd been given at the border and showed it to him.

"You are in the wrong place," he exclaimed after he examined the paper. "You must go to the building down the street."

Nadia asked the official some questions, and then we wished our English friends in line well and headed out the door.

The three of us climbed into a taxi and headed for the correct building. As we rode along, Nadia spoke to us. "There's a good chance you will be interviewed, but that's fine," she said. "Just answer the questions honestly and try not to be nervous. They may want to speak to you alone or together. Don't worry. Everything is going to work out."

The next building did not have the same cheerful atmosphere as the first. As we walked into the lobby, I noticed we were the only foreigners there. Nadia motioned for us to sit down on a wooden bench while she went and talked to an official. I could hear everything she was saying. She was telling the official behind the counter that we had come to collect our passports, which had been confiscated at the border.

"One moment, please," the official replied. "I will send someone to find the records."

Nadia thanked him and came and sat beside us on the bench. The three of us waited in silence. After about ten minutes an official asked Nadia and me to follow him. He led us into a small wood-paneled office furnished with a high-backed sofa and matching chairs.

"Be seated," he said before leaving the room.

Moments later a side door to the office swung open and in walked two Iranian men carrying notepads and pens. The older of the two men introduced himself as Mr. Akram, first to Nadia and then to me.

"Now, Mr. Baumann," he began as he sat down in one of the chairs opposite me, "can you tell us what nationality you are?"

"I am Swiss," I replied, and then I added, "But I was not born in Switzerland."

I waited for him to ask me if I was an American citizen, but he did not. Instead, he asked me questions about what I had done in Iran, if I wanted to come back to the country, and why I was presently living in Turkmenistan.

After nearly an hour of asking questions, Mr. Akram and the other man stood up. "That will be all, Mr. Baumann. Thank you for your time," he said, opening the door for us.

Nadia and I walked back into the lobby where Glenn was waiting anxiously for us. "How did it go?" he asked.

I turned to Nadia. "Fine," she replied. "I feel good about what happened. Do you?"

"Yes," I said. "They asked me a lot of pretty simple questions."

We all sat together on the bench for about fifteen minutes, then Mr. Akram and his assistant came and asked Glenn and Nadia to go with them into the same office I had been interviewed in. I was left sitting alone in the lobby. As I waited for them to return, I passed the time watching the lobby door, hoping to see other foreigners coming or going. I saw none, and I began to wonder what actually went on in this building.

Another hour dragged by, and eventually Glenn and Nadia, accompanied by Mr. Akram and his assistant, returned.

"Please wait here. We won't keep you long," Mr. Akram said as the two men disappeared back into the small office.

"How was it?" I asked Glenn when they were gone.

"Pretty good," he replied, then turning to Nadia, he added, "They were polite, eh? I don't think they want to spend any more time with us, do you?"

Nadia shook her head. "It all seemed fairly routine to me." She looked at her watch. "Hopefully, we'll be out of here by one, and you can catch a bus to Turkmenistan."

"Great," I replied. "Nothing would suit me more."

A few minutes later, Mr. Akram returned and asked Nadia to follow him into the office. Glenn and I sat waiting, expecting her to emerge at any moment with our passports in hand. When she finally walked out of the office, her face was ashen.

"Something is not right," she said in a hushed voice. "They say they are looking into something. I don't know what it is, but they told me they have to do more research. They want to interview each of you again, this time without me present."

"What does it mean?" I asked, my heart racing. "Did they give you any idea what they are looking into?"

Nadia shook her head. "None at all," she said. "But they say they'll be finished with you at 3 P.M. I think it would be best if I went back to the embassy and let them know what is happening here. I will be back at three o'clock to get you."

"But what should we say?" Glenn asked, more agitated than I had ever seen him. "What if they won't let us go?"

Nadia forced a smile. "It will be fine," she said, though not too convincingly. "They just want one more session with each of you. You both did fine before. Just tell them the truth, and they'll let you go."

Nadia stood up and walked out of the lobby.

As I watched her walk through the double glass doors, my heart sank. I wanted this whole ordeal to be over, but every step we took toward resolving it seemed to draw us into deeper trouble.

A few minutes later, I was called in for a second interview. This time, though, I was not led into the side office but was escorted upstairs to the second floor. The two men accompanying me swung open the door to a small room about eight feet by eight feet with a wooden desk and four old chairs in the middle of it. A tiny dirty window provided most of the light in the room, which was not much. I tried to think positively about the situation, but this dark room was not the sort of place where the government of Iran brought visitors to welcome them to the country! More ominous proceedings happened in dingy rooms like this, at least in the foreign spy movies I had seen.

Soon Mr. Akram and his assistant entered the room, and I heard the *click* of a key in the door lock.

"God, help me not to look nervous," I prayed under my breath.

Mr. Akram motioned for me to sit in the chair in front of the desk, while he, his assistant, and the two other men sat behind it. Suddenly he leaped to his feet and began yelling at me.

"Why are you here, Mr. Baumann? You will answer us truthfully this time!" he screamed into my face.

"I am here to learn about Iran and to see the countryside," I stammered, shocked at his sudden change in demeanor.

"Huh," Mr. Akram grunted, slamming a pad down in front of me. "List everything you have done while you've been in Iran. I want you to list every person you talked to, every place you visited, every home you stayed in. And leave nothing out."

For a moment I felt that I might throw up. Somehow, the worst possible scenario was playing itself out right before my eyes, and I was scared. How was I supposed to recall everything I had done in Iran with this man yelling in my face? I wrote for a few minutes, but Mr. Akram seemed to become bored watching me. Without warning, the yelling started again.

"Why do you live in Ashgabad?"

"I work for an organization that is looking for ways to help the people there," I replied vaguely, trying to keep the fear out of my voice that was tightening its grip on me.

"You can do better than that, Mr. Baumann!" Mr. Akram snapped. "We know exactly why you live in Ashgabad. In fact, we know a lot more about you than you think!" He reached across the desk and rammed a finger into my chest. "How about you start telling us the truth while we are still in a mood to listen to you. And you can begin with what you were doing in Afghanistan."

A warning went off in my head, and I realized that they did indeed know a lot more about me than I thought. I had not mentioned living in Afghanistan to them. I took a deep breath and said, "I went to

Afghanistan as a member of an international aid team. I worked there as an administrator for a hospital in Kabul."

When I finished answering, Mr. Akram threw the pad down in front of me again and yelled, "This time write down every country you have visited."

My heart sank. This list was going to look far more suspicious to them than anything else I had said or done so far. I picked up the pencil and began to write down the countries I had visited in Europe: Great Britain, the Netherlands, Sweden, Norway, Switzerland. I wrote slowly, hoping they would become bored watching me write before I got to some of the more controversial countries I had visited, like Israel. I was sure that one would raise even more questions and more yelling.

I wrote down ten countries, then twenty. I listed the countries of the Pacific I had visited. When I got to thirty countries, Mr. Akram interrupted me.

"So, Mr. Baumann, you have done a lot of traveling for an aid worker, wouldn't you say? Maybe now you will tell us where your money comes from?"

I looked at the extensive list on the pad, which was only half finished, and I had to admit I'd done a lot of traveling in my life. Except for the trips back to my parents' home countries as a child, I had visited all the other countries during various mission trips. I knew the only explanation that made any sense at all was the truth. "Well," I said, "you may be surprised to know that the money for my trips comes from several places. I am a Christian worker, and other Christians who believe in what I am doing send me money from time to time so I can go on trips."

A smug and satisfied smile spread across Mr. Akram's face, as if to say, *Now I have you.* "So what church do you belong to, Mr. Baumann? We have plenty of time. Tell us all about it," he demanded.

"My home church is called Calvary Church, in Los Angeles, California," I replied.

Mr. Akram then peppered me with questions: "How many people go there? What is the name of your pastor? How often do you report back to him? How many people does your pastor know in Washington? What are their names?"

Of course I had no idea how many people my pastor knew in Washington or who they were, and my inability to answer the question only infuriated my interrogator more.

"Mr. Baumann," he finally snapped, his face red and puffy, "since you will not tell us the truth, we will tell you. You were born in America. Your parents live in America. You are an American. You lie when you tell us you are a Swiss citizen!"

I pulled all of my concentration together and replied as deliberately as possible. "I am a Swiss citizen. I have been since I was born. But I am also an American citizen. However, I did not come here as an American. I came here on my Swiss passport."

By now it was three o'clock, and I was beginning to worry about how long they intended to hold me. This was not the simple question-and-answer session I had been told to expect by Nadia. I could sense something menacing about Mr. Akram. It was as if he took my Christian beliefs as a personal insult and was intent on crushing them. And now admitting I was an American citizen was sure to inflame the situation.

"So you are an American, Mr. Baumann! Where is your American passport?"

"Back in Turkmenistan," I answered.

"Why didn't you bring it with you?" Mr. Akram inquired.

"Because I am also Swiss. I used my Swiss passport. As you know, an American passport is not always welcome in this part of the world. It can cause problems."

"What do you mean problems?" he asked, pulling his face down level with mine.

I wanted to yell, "Like I'm having right now!" Instead, I said, "Sometimes visas are held up for Americans."

With my reply, Mr. Akram drew himself up straight, reached into his pocket, and pulled out my Swiss passport.

"Recognize this, Mr. Baumann?" he said with a snarl before slamming the passport down on the desk in front of me. Then in a loud voice that echoed around the room, he said, "All right, Mr. Baumann, enough pretending. Let's start again. Begin by telling us all the lies you have told us in the last few hours."

EIGHT

"What Are You Trying to Hide?"

A L L I wanted to do was curl up in a ball and take a rest, but the barrage of questions kept coming.

"We have lots of time," Mr. Akram taunted. "Now tell us the truth about where you purchased this passport."

Panicked thoughts raced through my head. Until now it hadn't occurred to me that they might not believe I was a dual citizen. "I am Swiss," I said, "and that is the truth."

Anger flashed across my interrogator's face. "You are not Swiss. Your parents live in America. You were born in America. You are an American," he hissed at me, slamming his fist into his hand at the same time.

The tension in the room was rising, and I knew he was thinking of smashing his fist into my face. For a moment I thought of taking my glasses off so they wouldn't get damaged if he got violent.

"Mr. Baumann, this is not the way to tell the truth!" he yelled while motioning for one of the other men in the room to get some handcuffs.

"You are not Swiss. You are an American," he yelled again. "If you cannot tell me the truth, you will be here for a very long time."

The yelling and threatening went on for well over an hour. No matter what I said, Mr. Akram refused to believe I was telling him the truth. As much as I wanted to tell him what he wanted to hear just to get out of there, I knew it would be dangerous to lie, and in the end it would only complicate matters when they questioned Glenn.

It was four o'clock when Mr. Akram finally turned to his assistant and said, "Enough!"

The men snatched up their papers and my passport and stormed out of the room. A soldier, who had evidently been stationed outside the door, walked in and sat down in one of the chairs. He kept his hand firmly on his gun and stared menacingly at me.

I grew so tired of being stared at that I closed my eyes. A maelstrom of disturbing thoughts tumbled around inside my head. Where was Glenn? Had he been released already? Would I be kept in custody now that I had confessed to being an American?

After I had put myself through ten minutes of self-torment, the soldier got up abruptly and motioned for me to follow him out the door.

We walked down the hallway and into a suite of rooms. He led me inside and then sat by the door. He waved his hand at me, and I took that to mean I could walk around. The room was a sparsely decorated lounge area, and next to it was an office with a desk and typewriter on it. At the far end of the office was a small bathroom. The suite had only one exit door, and that was the one the soldier was guarding.

I decided to sit in the office, where I could be alone with my thoughts and try to make some sense out of what was happening. It would also give me a chance to do some praying.

I was not alone for long, however. I heard the door open and then footsteps as Mr. Akram walked into the office. He looked frustrated and annoyed. I wondered if I was finally going to get hit this time.

He threw a stack of paper on the desk in front of me. "Okay, Mr. Baumann, it's time for you to get serious. You will stop playing games with us. Write down everything you've lied about in the last day. Give us a full account of why you came to Iran and detailed answers to all the questions we have asked you so far. What happens to you next depends on how cooperative you are."

Everything in me wanted to yell at him, "I am telling the truth. There's nothing more I can say." Instead, I held my breath and waited for him to leave.

A minute later I was sitting with the stack of paper in front of me, trying to think of what to write. I did not have the heart to begin, though. No matter what I wrote, I knew they would pick holes in it. And for some reason I did not understand, they were not willing to believe anything I had told them about being a Christian social worker.

I looked out the window, down two stories to the ground below. The alleyway at the back of the building was deserted. I could hear the honking of horns and the screeching of brakes in the distance as Tehran's evening rush hour got under way. As I looked down, I began to think of all the James Bond movies I had seen as a kid. I wondered what he would have done in my situation. Surely he wouldn't have sat idly by waiting for his interrogator to return.

I looked at the window again. It had a latch on it that allowed it to open wide enough for me to climb through. I got up and walked over to it. If I climbed out the window onto the ledge outside, I could turn my body around so I was facing the wall and then drop to the ground. I told myself two stories wasn't all that far to drop, and I could hit the ground running. With the money I had left in my pocket, I could hail a taxi and go straight to the South African embassy. I was in good physical shape, and I knew I would have a fair chance of making the escape. Yet as I sat there, I knew it was only a fantasy created by my tired mind. I had to stay and face whatever lay ahead. I had to trust God. I had no other choice.

At 5:30 P.M. Mr. Akram and his assistant returned. I was still sitting at the desk, trying to write. The serious consequences of making a single mistake caused my hands to shake so badly my words were barely legible.

"Is this all you have written?" Mr. Akram barked, looking down at the two paragraphs I had managed to produce.

"I can't write at the moment," I replied politely.

"Are you nervous? What are you trying to hide?" Mr. Akram retorted.

Here we go again, I thought. "No, it's not because I've done anything wrong," I said.

"Then why are you so nervous if you haven't done anything wrong?" he came right back at me. "What are you nervous about? Have we mistreated you?"

"No," I said. "I have not been mistreated."

"Is there something you do not wish us to know, Mr. Baumann? Something you are hiding perhaps?"

"No," I said. "I have told you everything about myself."

By then the sun had set, and a mantle of darkness enveloped Tehran as our conversation went round and round in circles. Then my interrogator abruptly changed tack. "Get up, Mr. Baumann. Let's go," he ordered.

I stood up and followed him and his assistant out of the room. The soldier followed behind us with his gun. We went down the stairs and along a corridor and back into the lobby area. To my amazement, Glenn walked into the lobby from a side room at the same time.

"They haven't let you go?" I blurted.

"No," he replied.

"I thought you were gone."

"Shut up!" Mr. Akram yelled in English. "Come with us, both of you," he continued in Farsi, motioning toward the main door of the building at the same time.

As we walked across the dimly lit lobby, three more men appeared from the shadows. Together the seven of us stepped outside. Mr. Akram and his assistant flanked us, and the other three men walked in front.

By now the night air was crisp and cold, and there were few cars and even fewer people in the street.

As we walked along silently, my mind swirled with questions: Where were we going? Were we about to be taken to the South African embassy? If not, how would Nadia or anyone else at the embassy find out where they were taking us? Why wouldn't they believe me when I said I held dual citizenship? Had they interrogated Glenn the same threatening way they had me? And if so, what about?

We had walked down the street about fifty yards when the three men in front led us around a corner. Lined up at the curb were three vehicles. Mr. Akram guided us toward the middle one. Glenn and I were forced by our captors to pull on blindfolds. Once in the vehicle, one of the men shoved my head down against the back of the front seat and told me not to lift it.

As we sped along through the streets of Tehran, I wondered where we were headed next. We didn't have to wait long, for within the hour we had been taken to a compound, stripped of our personal belongings, including my glasses, forced into long johns and pajamas that did not fit, and taken to the basement of the building. As we descended those stairs, the words that God had spoken to me only days before came to me vividly. "You are going to have to go to the bottom before you get out of here." Suddenly those words dawned with new meaning, and I began to pray that I would be faithful to Him, no matter what path I had to walk.

After walking down a long corridor that was dimly lit, the guard jerked my wrist for me to stop. I heard the rattle of keys in a lock and then the creaking of a door as it swung open. Suddenly, I felt myself being shoved from behind. I stumbled forward, trying to regain my balance. I heard the door slam shut behind me.

I reached up, took off my blindfold, and studied my new surroundings. I was in a cell about six feet wide and eight feet long. A scrap of thin carpet covered the tile floor, and an oil-heating radiator sat against the opposite wall. High in the top corner of the room was a small window. A blanket had been stuffed into it to try to stop the flow of cold air that seeped in through the opening, but the cell still had a damp chill to it.

Turning around I looked at the gray metal door. It had a mailbox-like opening in it about a foot from the ground. I paced back and forth for several minutes before sitting down on the carpet opposite the door. Inside, I was a swirl of raw and conflicting emotions. I wrapped my arms around my knees in an attempt to comfort and calm myself. It didn't work. The emotions, the questions, the doubts just kept washing over me. I was an American in jail in Iran. Images of the hostages at the United States embassy in Tehran nearly two decades before flooded through my mind. Surely I wouldn't have to suffer what they went through. Hopefully by now Nadia was aware of where we had been taken and had alerted the South African embassy. By tomorrow officials from the embassy would clear up the misunderstanding, and Glenn and I would be set free. Or so I hoped.

NINE

"Tell Me the Truth"

I HEARD a scuffling sound outside, and a metal tray of food was slid through a slot at the bottom of the door. On the tray was a pile of rice covered with beef *kofta*. I hadn't eaten anything since breakfast, so I was very hungry. I sat cross-legged on the floor and picked up the tray. My appetite soon disappeared, though, when I discovered the food was stone cold. Still, I forced myself to swallow a few pieces of beef and some rice. But instead of satisfying my hunger, the food made my stomach turn. I threw the rest of it into the trash can beside the door. I hoped I was disposing of it in the right way. Normally I didn't fret over such things, but I noticed I was becoming very concerned about doing the right thing and not making waves and giving my interrogator a reason to abuse me further.

I threw the tray in the corner of the cell and crawled over to the door. I put my ear next to the opening in the bottom and listened. I could hear one man talking to another. It sounded as though they were in different cells. A surge of hope shot through me. Maybe I could find Glenn!

"Glenn, Glenn, can you hear me?" I whispered as loudly as I dared and then held my breath and waited.

"Yeah," came a reply from down the corridor, sounding remarkably clear.

"How are you?" I asked.

"Okay," Glenn replied. "And you?"

"Not so good," I said. "I never thought it would turn out like this. Do you know what's going on?"

"No."

"Did they tell you how long you'd be in here?"

"No."

"Are you in a cell on your own?"

"Yeah."

"Me too," I said. "I have a feeling they're going to interrogate us again tomorrow."

Before Glenn could reply I heard footsteps marching toward my cell and then banging on the outside. The metal door vibrated against my ear.

"Silence! Now!" yelled a guard.

I crawled away from the door feeling triumphant. I had learned something the guards didn't want me to know: Glenn was okay and not far away.

After about fifteen minutes, I realized I needed to go to the bathroom. There was no toilet in my cell, so I got up and started banging on the door. I hoped it wouldn't anger the guards, but I couldn't think of what else to do. After a few minutes I heard a bunch of keys rattling, and then my cell door opened.

"What is it?" asked the guard roughly.

"I need the bathroom," I replied.

He grunted and pointed to a room opposite my cell. I walked over to it and opened the door. It was dingy inside, but I could see two toilets. Like most eastern toilets, they were basically holes in the ground. The room was divided, and I could hear a drip at the far end on the other side of the wall. I decided it was probably a shower.

When I was finished, the guard locked me back in my cell. To my horror, though, fifteen minutes later I had the urgent need to go again.

I'd only had one or two cups of water all day, but my nerves were getting the better of me. I ended up needing to go to the bathroom every fifteen minutes or so for the next two hours. With each trip, the guard became increasingly frustrated with me. It took him longer and longer to come to my cell when I banged on the door, and he cursed me each time he unlocked the door and let me out.

Finally, sometime around 2 A.M., the urge to use the bathroom finally subsided, and I was left alone with my thoughts. I thought through the day's events, looking for any clue as to what I had done to deserve the treatment I was receiving and for any sign of what might lie ahead. I tried to think of positive things to focus on, but no matter what directions my thoughts went in, eventually they came back to the cold and solitary cell I was trapped in. Everything about the situation made me want to escape its grim reality, but after every circle of wishful thought, I was still locked in a cold cell in a prison in Tehran, and I didn't know what was going to happen to us.

A few minutes later, I heard the guards change duty. After waiting fifteen minutes, I decided to see if I could talk to Glenn again. "Hey, Glenn, are you there?" I whispered into the hole in the bottom of the door.

"It's me," I heard the familiar whisper come back.

"I've been thinking," I said. "I'm going to tell them the truth 100 percent when they ask me something. There's no point in trying to hide anything. I just hope it doesn't get us killed."

"That's great, Dan. I've been thinking the same thing. We'll both tell the truth straight up, eh, and leave the outcome to God."

We talked for a few more minutes and then decided we should both try to get some sleep for whatever the next day held for us.

Sleep, though, did not come. It was easy to say we would leave the outcome to God, but I was finding it difficult to put into practice. I began to wonder if God was even there with me at all. Ever since I had been a young teenager, I'd felt God's presence with me. Although I loved to play group sports, I had been a loner at times. Once, at a fall youth camp when I was about sixteen, I stood alone next to a stream. I had some questions for God: Who was He, and what did He want with my life? As I stood at the water's edge throwing rocks, suddenly, out of nowhere, a strong impression came to me. It felt as though Jesus was standing right there with me, saying, "Don't make this complicated, Dan. I want to be your friend. If you want to throw rocks into the water, great. I'll be here throwing them with you." That night, when I went in for dinner, deep in my heart I knew God did not want me to be His robot on earth. He wanted to hang out with me and be my friend. And that's how it had been for most of my life.

Now, as I lay in my cold cell, I wondered where my Friend was. Thoughts and accusations came to me as rapidly as the guard's footsteps on the stone floor in the corridor outside my cell. "Where are you?" I asked, wiping hot tears from my cheeks. "Why did you allow this to happen to me?"

There was no answer.

"How long am I going to be here?" I finally asked out loud in despair.

Much to my surprise, a voice inside my head spoke. "You will be in here for nine weeks," the voice said.

I sat up straight, wide awake. I was horrified by the thought. It could not possibly be true! God wouldn't put me through nine weeks of hell like this, would He? Finally, I told myself that I was so upset by my circumstances that I was imagining things. I began to think of Lis, my older sister, and how she spent nine days in prison in Nepal. Maybe it would be the same for me. God knew that was about all I could take without seeing the sun or talking to my parents on the phone.

The thought of my parents made me begin to cry. I soon curled up in a ball and sat there sobbing uncontrollably.

I had been crying for only a few minutes when the light in my cell went on. Teary eyed I crawled to the door and peered through the hole. Suddenly loud chanting echoed through my cell, and I leaped back from the door. By getting down low to the ground, I was able to see that a loudspeaker had been positioned right outside my cell.

How could I have forgotten? Today was the first day of Ramadan, the holy month when all Muslims fasted from sunrise to sunset. No wonder the prison had come alive so early. Soon a guard was standing in front of my cell.

"Stand away from the door," a harsh voice yelled.

I obeyed, and the cell door swung open.

"Do not look out," the voice said, now emanating from an elderly man with a pronounced limp.

In one hand he held a metal plate with one piece of bread, a blob of jelly, and a square of feta cheese, and in the other a mug of strong black tea. He looked impatiently at me, and I quickly reached out and took the plate and the mug from him. I placed them on the floor and quickly handed him the empty food tray from the night before.

"What time is it?" I asked.

He glanced at his watch. "Three o'clock," he replied before slamming my cell door shut behind him.

While it wasn't over yet, this night had already turned out to be the longest night of my life. I sat down in the same spot where I had eaten the night before and placed the plate in front of me. I smeared the jelly onto the bread as best I could with my finger and took a bite. It was stale and hard, so I dipped it in my tea. The tea seemed to mask the staleness, and the bread was soon gone. Still hungry, I picked up the feta cheese to eat, but its strong pungent smell made my nervous stomach gag, and so I tossed it in the trash can.

What was left of the night passed slowly. I peered out through the tiny corner of the window not obscured by the blanket that had been stuffed in it. The pale light spilling in told me dawn was beginning to break. As the sun rose, the monotonous chanting seemed to go on interminably. I soon developed a migraine headache, the combined result, I was sure, of the chanting, not wearing my glasses, lack of sleep, and constant worry.

As best I could tell, it was about eleven o'clock when the door of my cell burst open and two guards walked in.

"Put on your blindfold and come with us," the taller guard said.

I did as I was told and was led into the hallway. As we walked down the corridor, I peered through the bottom of my blindfold and noticed a room with large bloodstains on the ground and an electronic switchboard with electrodes. Horrid images of the torture that must have gone on there filled my tired mind. I was relieved when I passed that room and was led into another one.

"You can take your blindfold off now, Mr. Baumann," a voice said.

A shiver ran down my spine. I immediately recognized the voice as that of Mr. Akram, my interrogator from the day before.

I took off the blindfold as instructed and looked around. I was in a large room with four chairs gathered around a table in the center with a portable heater in the corner. Mr. Akram was sitting in one of the chairs.

"Take a seat," he said.

I sat down in the chair he pointed to and looked down at the tiled floor. I froze with fear. Beneath my chair was a huge pool of dried blood. Someone sitting right where I was had bled profusely. Probably while being beaten to death, I told myself. I tried not to look down again.

"Hello, Mr. Baumann," Mr. Akram began in an oily voice. "Did you have a good night? Did you sleep well?"

"I've slept better," I replied.

"Here are your glasses. I'm sure you have missed them."

He leaned over and handed them to me, and I quickly put them on.

"Is there anything that was not provided in your cell that I might be able to get for you?" he asked.

I wanted to laugh out loud. He could start with a comfortable bed, a decent toilet, and an honest explanation as to why I was in prison! "No, I'm fine for now," I finally managed to say.

"Good, then we can get down to business, can't we?" he continued, pulling a pad and pen out of his briefcase. "Now, I want you to answer some simple questions for me, okay?"

"Okay," I said, dreading a repeat of the day before.

"When did you come to Iran?"

"December 27, 1996," I said.

"Very good, and what was your main reason for coming here?"

I winced for a moment. I thought about my conversation with Glenn during the night about being totally honest, and then I remembered the pool of dried blood beneath my chair. *God, help me to convey your love to these men,* I prayed silently and then took a deep breath before speaking. "I am in Iran to tell you about Jesus. Yes, I am here as a tourist, and yes I have come to see if I can help develop trade ties, but

I have deep convictions, and those convictions are, first and foremost, what brought me to Iran."

Mr. Akram put down his pen and drew closer to me. "And what are your deep convictions, Mr. Baumann?"

"I believe that Jesus Christ is the only Son of God, and that out of deep love for us He died on the Cross so we can all find our way back to God."

Mr. Akram laughed scornfully. "Why would you believe that?" he asked.

Although he laughed, he sounded ready to hear more, so I went on to tell him about how God wants to change lives and bring peace and joy.

"How interesting," Mr. Akram commented dryly. "And now you might like to tell us who really funds these little trips of yours, Mr. Baumann."

"Sure," I said, feeling a little less intimidated by the dried blood beneath my chair. "I have many friends who believe in what I'm doing. They give me a little money, and my church gives me a little money, and I live very simply, as you know. I stay with friends or in cheap local hotels, and I eat local food."

"So your church provides you with money, does it? And what does it ask of you in return for this money they give you?"

"Only that I try to help people wherever I go, and that when I get the opportunity, I tell them Jesus loves them," I replied. I knew it would sound incredibly unbelievable to any Muslim, but I was determined to only tell the truth and leave the consequences to God. I had already taken the plunge, and there was no turning back.

"And you did this while you were in Afghanistan?" Mr. Akram asked.

"Yes," I replied.

"Tell me how exactly you did this job your church paid you to do, Mr. Baumann."

The more I talked, the more faith welled up inside of me. The chorus "Walk in the Light Where God Is" kept running through my mind, and I knew as long as I followed the chorus's admonition, I had nothing to fear. After about twenty minutes of listening to me talk about the hospital I administered in Afghanistan, Mr. Akram appeared to get bored. He interrupted me and changed topics.

"Now, Mr. Baumann, that sounds all well and good, but don't you think it's time to get honest with us? You are not Swiss. Please stop talking about being Swiss. We are over that. You have lied. Next time when we ask who you are, you will say, 'I am an American.'"

"And a Swiss," I interjected, watching the veins bulge in Mr. Akram's neck as his eyes narrowed.

"Take off your glasses, Mr. Baumann," he screamed.

My hands trembled as I slid them off and placed them on the table in front of me. The old cliché "never hit a man with glasses" ran through my mind.

Wham! A heavy blow caught the right side of my face.

"Come on, Mr. Baumann, you can do much better than that. It's time to tell us the truth."

"I have told you the truth as much as I can," I said through clenched teeth.

Whack! Another blow slammed into my face. My eyes began to water, and my teeth throbbed.

"Tell us what CIA stands for, Mr. Baumann."

"Central Intelligence Agency," I replied.

"Ha," Mr. Akram yelled, stepping back. "Now we are getting somewhere! How would a social worker know something like that? Huh?"

I wanted to laugh at the absurdity of his comment, but I knew it would only inflame the situation and earn me another blow to the face. "Everyone in America knows what CIA stands for," I said. "It's even in movies."

"You work for the CIA. Admit it," he demanded, slapping me again.

Jesus' words in Matthew 5:44 came to me right then. "Pray for them which despitefully use you, and persecute you" (KJV).

"You are lying. Every American foreigner works for the CIA. It is your patriotic duty!"

"Well, I don't work for them, sir," I said.

"Don't lie to me," he yelled as he raised his hand again.

Slap!

"Tell me the truth."

Slap!

The conversation went on for fifteen or twenty more slaps, until my cheeks were swollen and my head felt as if it would burst.

"Put your blindfold back on, Mr. Baumann," Mr. Akram hissed. "We will have another talk like this soon, and I hope you will be more cooperative then."

I heard him pick up my glasses from the table as a guard led me away.

The door of my cell slammed shut behind me, and I took off my blindfold gingerly. I wished I had a mirror to examine the damage to my face, but as I ran my fingers over it, it felt tight and swollen. I sat down in the corner and let the tears flow. I was sure Glenn would be next, and I prayed for him between sobs. "God, give him the strength to love these people and to tell the truth no matter how much they abuse him."

As I prayed, a peace came over me. In a strange way I felt liberated. The one thing all Americans working in Muslim countries feared might happen to them was happening to me. I was being held in prison without any explanation. I was being interrogated and physically abused, and yet I could feel God's presence there with me. And that feeling made everything I was going through seem bearable. I remembered my prayer to God and reminded myself that I had to trust that He had a purpose for what was happening. I didn't understand, but I knew I had to rely on Him to bring me through.

I sat for about two hours with my back against the wall, thinking of Jesus' Sermon on the Mount. "Blessed are you when people insult you, persecute you and falsely say all kinds of evil against you because of me. Rejoice and be glad, because great is your reward in heaven, for in the same way they persecuted the prophets who were before you."

The simplicity and the power of Jesus' sermon overwhelmed me.

Around midafternoon, I heard the guards outside my cell again. I felt my stomach tighten. Was I going back to Mr. Akram for another session?

I put on my blindfold and was led from my cell down the corridor. As I walked, I could hear one man in a cell muttering to himself and another chanting. As I stepped into the interrogation room again, I heard the sound of Mr. Akram's now familiar and terrifying voice.

"Take off your blindfold, Mr. Baumann."

I took if off and sat down in the same chair I had sat in only several hours before.

"Now that you have had some time to think about it, maybe you would like to tell us the truth."

"I have told you the truth all along, sir," I responded.

Whack! The first blow hit me on the left side of my face this time. My brain registered the pain, but a question ran through my mind. *Lord, what do you think of Mr. Akram and these people?*

"I love them," I felt He replied.

Despite my desperate circumstance, my heart was broken with a God who loved all His children without conditions and wanted a relationship with each one. Again I felt a peace come over me, and it must have registered on my face, because after his third blow Mr. Akram stopped and looked at me.

"What are you thinking, Mr. Baumann?" he demanded.

I gulped. "This may sound crazy," I said, "but I do love you."

The three people in the room all started to laugh.

"You're crazy!" Mr. Akram said, slapping me again. "You're an idiot."

"No," I said, when he let up on me for a moment, "I'm not crazy. I have the Holy Spirit inside me, and He wants you to know Jesus as I do. Once you know Jesus, it's possible to love even your enemies."

"Ha," he snorted. "No wonder the West is so weak! What a crazy story!"

"Mr. Akram," I continued, looking him directly in the eye, "you can hit me all day long, and I will love you. But much more important than that, Jesus Christ loves you."

"Shut up," he yelled. "Just shut up."

He sat down behind the desk and handed me my glasses again. Apparently the blows were over for now. I slid the glasses on, though they balanced precariously on my swollen, puffy face.

Mr. Akram then began asking me the same questions he had asked that morning and the day before. Did I belong to the CIA? What was my church really paying me to do in Iran? Why did I insist on pretending I was Swiss? Could I account for every minute I had spent in Iran? Where did my money really come from? What contacts did my pastor have in Washington, D.C.?

This circular rhythm of questions and answers went on for over an hour, then once again my glasses were confiscated and I was led blindfolded back to my cell.

I felt an odd surge of relief as the door shut behind me. In my mind, my cell, which I had hated at first, had been transformed into a place of safety and refuge. No one was going to hit me in there or yell at me. No one was going to tell me I was an idiot or a liar or working for the CIA. That last thought scared me because I knew if they were convinced I worked for the CIA, the consequences could cost me my life.

By now it was late afternoon, and I sat down beside the door so I could see the tiny patch of sky through the corner of the window. As I watched the clouds roll by, I thought of Job, who in the Old Testament had questioned why God let bad things happen to him. "God," I prayed out loud, "no matter what happens to me, I don't want to curse you. Even if I am here for the rest of my life, I never want to question you. But I am weak, and I am scared that is exactly what I'll do. Please help me so I do not dishonor your name."

"This Is Your Last Chance, Mr. Baumann"

EVENTUALLY the pale yellow sunlight in the corner of my cell window faded, and I heard the sound of a man coming down the corridor. I hoped it was dinnertime, because I had hardly eaten any of the food they had brought me the last time.

Sure enough, the cell door swung open and there stood the old man. This time he held a tray loaded with rice, beef kofta, a gray meat stew, and two flatbreads, along with a mug of hot tea. I took the tray and mug from him and handed over the metal plate and empty mug from breakfast. I thanked him for the food and tea and sank down in the corner of the cell that had become my dining area.

The loud chanting had continued to be played over the loudspeaker outside my cell door throughout the day, and dinnertime was no exception. I ate my food to the accompaniment of a loudly chanting mullah.

Finally, at about ten o'clock in the evening, the loudspeaker fell silent. I crawled to the door and sat by it for a while, wondering if I dare call out to Glenn. Part of me didn't want to call. What if he wasn't there? What would I do? And what if he had been badly beaten, too? How would I be able to comfort him? It took me a long time, but in the end I summoned the courage to whisper through the slot in the bottom of the door. "Glenn, are you there?"

"Yeah, it's me," came the reply.

"Did they interrogate you?" I asked.

"Yeah, I got slapped around a bit. How about you?"

"Me too. Are you okay?"

"No broken bones, but I'm tired of being asked the same questions all the time."

"So am I," I responded. "I'm a nervous wreck now, but when I was with Akram, I felt a power going through me. I tell you, the apostle Paul was right. The Holy Spirit gave me the words to say, and I told Akram exactly why we were here."

"Isn't it amazing!" Glenn replied. "The very same thing happened to me. Dan, it's a good thing we're both committed to telling the truth, because it sure makes it easy for our answers to match, eh?"

"You're right about that," I said.

Just then I heard a guard kick my door, and I stopped talking. As I wrapped a woolen blanket around me, I knew that somehow, in the midst of all of this madness, God was with me and was giving me courage.

My racing thoughts kept me awake most of the night. But I managed to get about two hours sleep before it was breakfast time again, signaling the start of my second full day in prison. I fervently hoped that it would be my last. Surely, I told myself, my captors could not keep asking me the same questions endlessly. What purpose did it serve?

At about eleven o'clock, the same routine as the day before repeated itself: the guard, the blindfold, and Mr. Akram waiting for me. This time, though, he did not go into his normal welcoming banter. Instead, he began a tirade as soon as I entered the room, angrily berating me for working with the CIA.

"I want the names of all of your connections!" he yelled as I took off my blindfold.

"I don't know anyone from the CIA," I said, trying not to sound as frustrated as I felt.

"Of course you do," he snapped back. "We know for a fact you have American embassy connections in Kabul and Ashgabad. You have been in the embassy in both cities, haven't you?"

"Well, yes," I agreed. "I have been to those embassies and spoken to people there. But they were not CIA agents, only clerks I talked to about my visas and the necessary papers I needed to travel there."

"India!" Mr. Akram screamed at me. "You know CIA agents in India, too. It's no use denying it, Mr. Baumann."

By now I wanted to scream, too. There seemed to be no way to convince my interrogator I was telling the truth. He wanted me to be a CIA spy, and he wasn't going to stop badgering me until I confessed to being one. And if I succumbed to their pressure and told them what they wanted to hear, I knew the consequences could mean rotting away for the rest of my life in a dark prison cell in Iran or even death, whatever served their political ambitions the best.

After a few more minutes of aggressive questioning, Mr. Akram changed tack. He smiled widely and then said softly, "Dan, let's make a deal."

"What do you want?" I asked.

"Why don't you become a double agent?"

"What do you mean a double agent?" I inquired.

"Well, we know you work for people in the CIA, and we have a letter we need to get to the CIA people. If you want, you can deliver it for us. If you agree to do this, you will be out of here within twenty-four hours with no more questions asked."

"How can I be a double agent? I don't work for our government!" I said, despairing he had not believed a single word I'd spoken up till now.

"Think about it, Dan. Think about it," Mr. Akram said quietly. "This could be your only ticket out."

We talked for a while longer, and I decided to be noncommittal about the whole idea. I desperately wanted to get back to my cell to think about what I was being told. I needed to work out what kind of trap Mr. Akram was laying for me. We eventually parted on a "friendly" note, and I was led back to my cell.

I spent a lot of time thinking and praying about what had happened during that time of interrogation, and I wasn't surprised later in the afternoon when Mr. Akram stepped into my cell. He looked relaxed and happy to see me. I scrambled to my feet.

"Have you thought about it, Mr. Baumann?" he said enthusiastically. "Have you thought about my offer?"

I didn't say anything. I couldn't see any point.

Mr. Akram stroked his short-clipped black beard. "Well, is there anything I can do for you while you think about it?" he asked.

"Yes," I said, deciding to make the most of his offer. "You can give me my Bible and my glasses."

"No problem, Mr. Baumann," he said brightly. "They will be delivered to you soon." He smiled one last time and left my cell.

Half an hour later, the cell door opened again, and a guard handed me my glasses and my maroon hardcover Bible.

I slid on my glasses and held the Bible for a while, almost afraid to break the spell of the moment by opening it. Eventually, I flicked through its pages to the book of Psalms. I read and meditated on the words I found there until the lights finally went out for the night.

The following morning, I was blindfolded again. Once I was in the corridor, though, the guard led me in the opposite direction this time. This change in routine upset me. I was becoming a little more "institutionalized" each day and relied on the familiarity of turning right when I was taken out of my cell, even if it did lead to Mr. Akram and his abuse. But now my institutionalized world had been turned upside down. I was being taken to the left.

A short distance along the corridor, I was led into a room and told to take off my blindfold. As my eyes adjusted to the bright overhead lighting, I saw I was standing in a plush office. Mr. Akram sat behind a large mahogany desk, and I wondered if this was his private office.

"Okay, Dan, let's get down to work," he said in a friendly voice, almost as if I were in the office for a job interview. He slid a pad and pen across the desk toward me. "Just tell us your CIA activities for the last two weeks, and everything will go fine for you. You will be out of here very soon."

"I can't. I'm not a member of the CIA," I said.

"What do you mean?"

"I've told you many times already that I'm not with the CIA."

Mr. Akram's friendly tone quickly changed to a menacing one. "Mr. Baumann, do you know what's going to happen to you if you do not comply?"

"No," I replied, yet inside I feared the worst.

"Do you know you could be our guest..." he paused for dramatic effect, "...for a very long time?"

"I can't help that," I said. "What else can I say? I am not with the CIA, and I don't know anyone who is. If I did I'd deliver the letter for you, but since I don't, I can't."

"What a pity, Mr. Baumann," Mr. Akram said. "There is only one more way for you to get out of here. If you give me fifty thousand American dollars, I could release you tomorrow."

I laughed out loud. "Where do you think I could get that much money?" I asked.

"What do you mean, where could you get that much money? It's nothing to you! I know what's in your account in America. I know how much you people make. Stop playing games with me and be sensible. Help yourself while you can!" He thumped his fist on the desk for added emphasis.

"Maybe I could come up with two thousand dollars, but that would be about it," I countered.

This time Mr. Akram laughed. "Then you can expect to be seeing me for a very long time." And with a serious note he added, "This is your last chance, Mr. Baumann. Are you going to confess or not?"

"I can't confess," I said wearily. "I have nothing to confess to."

"Okay, you have made your choice," he said, opening his hands. He turned to the guard and ordered, "Take this prisoner back to his cell."

I had just settled down into the corner of my cell when the door swung open again, and a different guard stepped inside. "Give me your glasses and that book," he demanded.

My heart sank, but I had no choice other than to hand them over.

With nothing to read to take my mind off the last interrogation session, I began to replay the events of the last two days in my mind. Did Akram seriously think I was a CIA agent? Did he really want me to confess so he could let me go? And what did he mean when he said, "This is your last chance"? Was something bad about to happen to me soon?

I thought back to the chilling story a staff member at the South African embassy had told Glenn and me the day before we were taken as prisoners. Apparently, one of the other staff members at the embassy, an Iranian woman, had a son who was interested in the Turkmen people. He had been warned several times not to do any research on them or contact them. He was told the lives of the Turkmen were not to be documented in any way. The son had gone ahead anyway, asking discreet questions and visiting Turkmen people in their *yurts*.

One afternoon, when the embassy worker and her husband were at home together, someone knocked at the door. The woman opened the door, and standing there were two Iranian police officers. They pushed past her and into the living room, carrying a black trash bag between them. Without a word, they dumped the bag on the floor and left. When the couple opened the bag, they recoiled in shock. Inside was the body of their son cut into pieces.

Nothing more was ever said about the death, though the woman never recovered completely from the devastating shock of her son's brutal murder.

As I thought about the story, the serious trouble Glenn and I were in became very clear to me. Not only had we admitted to telling Iranians about our faith in Jesus, a serious offense itself in Iran, but our captors also had all our notes in their possession, and they clearly showed our interest in the Turkmen people.

I began to consider the possibility that "a last chance to confess" meant I was going to be killed soon, probably by hanging, which in a macabre moment, I decided I would prefer to a firing squad.

As I sat in my cell, I discovered one thing worse than thinking about the possibility of being killed. That was letting my mind drift off to think about my family and friends. Sure, it was pleasant to think about my mom and dad and wonder what they were doing at that moment, or whether my younger sister had given birth to her baby yet. I even wondered what I would be doing if I were at home in Colorado. Maybe I'd be playing golf with a buddy or hiking in the mountains with a group of friends. These thoughts offered a pleasant escape from my current circumstance for a few moments. But when my mind returned to focus on the present, I was still in my cell, scared and alone, and feeling ten times worse than I did before I had started thinking about home. I tried to discipline my mind to concentrate only on my situation within the prison walls. It was the only way I knew to stop the cycles of depression I found myself going through. It was not easy, though. The alluring pull of escaping into thoughts of home and family and friends was almost irresistible.

It was about 5 P.M. when another guard appeared at the door of my cell and told me to put on my blindfold. I didn't know what to expect. The only thing I was reasonably sure of was that I wasn't going to another one of Akram's interrogation sessions. I believed him when he said I'd had my last chance.

The guard led me back to the first room I had been interrogated in, the one with the dried blood on the floor. As I took off my blindfold, the first person I saw sitting in the room was Glenn. I was so relieved to see him, I wanted to throw my arms around him. He looked in reasonably good shape except for a small cut under his left eye.

"How are you?" I asked.

"Okay," he replied. "God has been good, eh?"

"He sure has," I replied.

The guard who brought me into the room pointed to two black trash bags. "Get dressed," he said in Farsi.

"He's telling us to get dressed," I relayed to Glenn as I grabbed the nearest bag. I pulled it open and inside were my clothes. "This looks positive," I said as I began to strip off my prison pajamas.

"Yeah, let's hope for the best, eh?" Glenn said.

It felt so good to get out of the prison uniform and back into my own clothes. My watch and glasses were in the bag, too. When I was dressed, the guard thrust a pen and a sheet of paper at me. It was the same sheet on which I had listed all of my belongings when I first arrived at the prison. Everything was there just as I had left them, even my wallet with all of the money in it. I signed the sheet and waited for Glenn to check his belongings and do the same.

"Blindfolds back on," the guard barked.

I took off my glasses and slipped them into my shirt pocket before pulling on my blindfold for what I hoped was the last time.

A guard took hold of my arm and led me down the corridor, up ten steps, and out a large door into the cool night air. I breathed deeply before once again my head was pushed down and I was told to get into a car. Out the corner of my blindfold, I saw what appeared to be the same Nissan Patrol that had brought us to the prison. I took it as another good sign, though I didn't know why. Glenn climbed into the vehicle beside me.

"Get down," the guard said.

Glenn and I obeyed immediately, tucking our heads between our knees. As we did so, we reached out and linked our arms together for support and encouragement. Could we really be on our way to freedom?

Room 58

"I T ' S January fifteenth, isn't it?" I whispered to Glenn as we rode along.

"I think so," he replied. "Do you think they're letting us go?"

"Let's hope so," I said.

I listened intently as our vehicle drove out through the prison gate checkpoint and into the general flow of traffic. Cars and trucks honked, and brakes screeched all around us. Amid all the noise, I searched for clues that might give some indication of where we were headed.

The vehicle drove on for about thirty minutes until it slowed down and then finally stopped. I could hear the driver wind down his window and talk to someone outside.

I decided we must be at another type of checkpoint and lifted my head slowly, hoping to catch a glimpse of where we were. I reached up and adjusted my blindfold so I could see out of the left corner of it. That was when my heart sank. We were outside another large and ominous-looking compound. The red-brick walls surrounding it were high, and it had solid metal gates. Several guards stood around the car.

I ducked my head again. "It doesn't look good," I whispered to Glenn. "We're probably at another prison."

Glenn didn't reply, and the two of us sat shoulder to shoulder, wrapped up in our own thoughts for several minutes.

When all the official paperwork was taken care of, the gates swung open and the driver maneuvered the vehicle forward before bringing it to a halt in a large courtyard. As I climbed out, I caught a glimpse of a garden area to my left. Although I could only see a small portion of the structure around us, I had the impression this facility was a much larger place than the prison we had just left.

Once we were outside the vehicle, the routine we had gone through to exit the first prison was now reversed. We were guided up some stairs, taken into a small room, and told to take off our blindfolds and start undressing. When I took off my blindfold, everyone around me was either wearing a guard's uniform or the telltale striped prison pajamas.

I was handed another trash bag, though this one had a bright yellow ribbon on top to seal it, and told to put all my clothes except my underwear in it. Once again I had to make a list of all my personal items I put in the bag and then sign it. I didn't offer to put my glasses in, and much to my relief, no one told me to. One of the guards stepped up and put my toothbrush and asthma inhaler on a separate bench. I hoped that meant they would stay with me in the cell.

After I was undressed, another guard handed me a pair of wooly long johns and an undershirt. As before, they were both too small for me. The long johns were several inches too short in the legs, but I struggled into them, knowing that if I complained, I might not have any to wear at all. After I had squeezed into the long johns, one of the guards handed me some striped pajamas to put on, along with a pair of orange plastic sandals.

Glenn was also forcing himself into a prison uniform obviously too small for him. As we both dressed, the two guards who had escorted us from the other prison left the room, leaving us in the care of four guards we had never seen before. One of them, an older man with weathered features and a hint of kindness curled up at the corners of his mouth, reached into my plastic sack and pulled out my wallet. He took twenty thousand rial from the wallet and laid the money beside my toothbrush. "You will need this," he said, putting the wallet back into my bag.

"Thank you," I said, wondering what I could possibly need money for in a place like this.

All the while, I kept my Bible beside me. I hoped there was a way I could keep it with me and not have to put it into the bag. I looked at the guards. They all seemed friendly and relaxed, but one of them, a man about forty-five, had a particularly open and kind-looking face. He was obviously not the head guard, but I felt that if anyone could help me he would. I decided to appeal to him. "You know, sir," I said, looking right at him, "I am a Christian, and I read my Bible every day. I would like to keep it with me, just as a devout Muslim would like to have the Koran with him at a time like this."

The guard looked startled, as if he could hardly believe I was talking to him. Then he looked away. Had I seen him nod his head slightly or not? I couldn't tell.

"Put it in the bag," he finally said after a moment of indecision.

I did as I was told, and then I sat on a narrow wooden bench and waited. Sitting scrunched up on the bench made my prison pajamas look ridiculously small. The legs came halfway up my calves.

Outside the room, I could hear people having what seemed to be one-way conversations. After a moment or two, I realized they were talking on the telephone. I guessed we must be in some sort of administration wing.

A minute later, another guard came into the room and told me to stand up. It was time to go. He motioned for me to pick up my toothbrush, inhaler, and the money. I shot Glenn one last look as I put on my blindfold and held out my arm to be led away.

We walked down a corridor and turned left. Through the corners of my blindfold, I could make out solid metal doors on both sides. I knew I was being led to another cell. It was almost the same as the prison I had just left, except beside each door was a shelf with a small basket on it containing a few personal possessions of each prisoner.

The corridor opened into a large area. I could just make out the phosphorous glow of a wall of TV screens. I squinted hard to see what was on the screens. To my horror they showed pictures of empty prison corridors. I realized whatever this place was, it was high security and high tech.

The guard pulled me to a stop outside a cupboard. After unlocking the cupboard door, he pulled down my blindfold. "Take one," he said, pointing to the pile of gray blankets inside.

My feet were so cold that I reached in and grabbed not one but four blankets. I held my breath, waiting to be yelled at for disobeying an order, but the guard didn't seem to care how many blankets I took. I tucked them under my arm, pulled up my blindfold, and waited to be led on. We walked for a few more yards straight ahead and then made a right turn. It wasn't until I got to the end of another corridor that the guard stopped me and pulled down my blindfold.

"Room 58," he said. "Remember that number. That's who you are."

I nodded.

"Put your things in there." He pointed to the small basket on the shelf outside the door.

Once again I was disappointed. I wasn't going to get to keep my toothbrush or my inhaler after all. As the control of my life was stripped away, somehow the smallest things that I could keep became a solace to me, but that would not be the case here either. Reluctantly I put them into the basket and watched as the guard swung open the cell door to reveal my new home.

It was about the same size as my previous cell. A single light bulb, encased in wire mesh, shed a harsh light on the room. I instinctively looked at the floor covering, since there was no bed in the room. The carpet, no thicker than a towel, was frayed and worn.

The guard turned and left, locking the door behind him. I was alone again.

I surveyed the cell some more. A red plastic trash basket and a jug with a wide spout were sitting on the floor. In the middle of the floor was a metal bowl of soup and a spoon, my dinner for the night. To the right of the door was a stainless steel sink and toilet with no seat. I turned on the faucets, and to my surprise, they ran with both hot and cold water. I stood for a moment and let the warm water run over my hands. It was a simple luxury, but it felt good. On one side of the sink were two bars of soap. On the wall opposite the door was a metal screen with a heating radiator behind it.

I sat down on the tattered carpet and unfolded my new plastic tablecloth in preparation for dinner. I caught a smell of the food, and it almost made me want to throw up. Still, I forced myself to swallow a couple of spoonfuls. The taste was fouler than the smell, and I threw the rest of it down the toilet. I went to flush it away, but when I pushed the flusher nothing happened. It was then that I realized what the plastic jug was for. I had to fill it three or four times before I had enough water to swish away the food.

Once I had flushed away my dinner, I turned to face the door. Above it was a window with frosted glass and large metal bars across it. The door was metal, too, and at about eye level, there was a hole, but no slot at the bottom as there had been in the door of my previous cell.

I tried to keep my attention on the door for as long as I could, studying every scratch and paint chip. I knew it would be a mistake to examine everything in the room too fast. Once everything had been looked at, what would I do then?

After a minute or two, I stepped over to the trash can and noticed something in the bottom. I picked up the basket and slowly reached in. Two cigarette packs had been discarded by some previous prisoner. I pulled them out and flipped them open. They were both empty, but I examined them closely just to occupy my mind. The black label on the outside of each pack read, "Montana, made in Mexico," and I wondered why they didn't use Iranian cigarettes in the prison.

After examining the empty cigarette packs, I moved on to count the sets of tally marks scratched into the wall. There were ten sets of them, most scratched into the wall opposite the sink and toilet. The smallest amount tallied was two, and the largest amount twenty-six. They were obviously left by prisoners who had been assigned to room fifty-eight before me. No doubt they marked off the number of days each man had spent in this cell. I thought about the person who had spent only two days in the cell. What had happened to him? Had he been executed after two days? And what about the person who had spent twenty-six days in the cell? Was twenty-six days the longest time

the authorities would keep a person locked up here? My mind desperately wanted to latch on to some piece of information that could give
some clue as to how long I might be detained here. Being in solitary
confinement was wearing down my nerves, and I didn't know how
much more I could take.

Finally, I decided it was time to lie down, though I was sure I
wouldn't sleep. I took two of the blankets and folded them over twice
so they were about a foot wide and an inch thick. Then I laid the two
blankets side by side to form a makeshift mattress. I ran them diago-
nally across the cell, since that was the only way I would be able to
stretch out properly. The blankets were unusually long, and I was able
to roll the top of them up and slide my two sandals inside to form a
pillow.

Once the "bed" was made, I climbed in, pulling the other two
blankets over me. My head butted up against the wall, and my feet
were tucked in the corner against the metal screen. As I lay there, terrifying thoughts overtook me. I thought about the previous prison
and longed to go back there. I missed the routine. I missed the food
and the familiar sounds of the men in the next cells. I missed being
able to whisper through the door to Glenn at the other end of the corridor. In a weird sort of way, I even missed the thought of not seeing
Mr. Akram again. Even though he had beaten and tormented me, he
had been another human being to talk to. I felt an irrational bond with
him that I couldn't explain.

Over the next several hours I could hear guards walking up to my
door and then see them peering at me through the hole. Looking up
into their staring faces made me feel like an animal in a cage.

The first "friendly" face I saw was the cigarette man, who came by
my cell at 8 P.M. I got up as I heard him unlock the door. He carried a
wooden tray with stacks of cigarettes neatly lined up on it. He
motioned for me to take a cigarette, but I shook my head. He nodded
at me, and I thought I saw his lips turn up into a slight smile as he
shut the door behind him. I hoped that maybe he wanted to be my
friend.

Not long after the cigarette man left, I heard the rattling of a cart
outside, and the candy man arrived at my cell door. I held out my plate,

and he put a hard candy on it. I thanked him and sat down, staring at my piece of candy. It was red, and I wondered what flavor it was. I ran through the flavor options of all the red candy I had eaten in the past: cherry, raspberry, strawberry, even apple. Which flavor was this candy? After studying it for a minute or two, I decided to end the suspense. I lifted the candy to my lips and dropped it into my mouth. It was cherry flavored.

I was just taking the last few sucks on the candy when the loud-speaker outside my cell door crackled to life and prayer chants began to play. The sound seemed to echo around my cell, bouncing off the concrete walls. I sat and waited for it to end. When it finally died away, I decided to ask for my toothbrush. I hadn't cleaned my teeth in three days, and I hoped that if I asked the guard nicely, he might let me use it.

As it turned out, the guard who came when I banged on the door also offered to sell me some toothpaste for seven hundred and fifty rial. I gladly bought it with some of my money.

The guard put the toothpaste on the brush for me and then handed it to me. I felt as though I were four years old again. The toothpaste had a strong peppermint taste and smell, but it was course and gritty. It felt like sand on my teeth. Still, I was grateful for it and brushed a long time before rinsing my mouth out and handing the brush back to the guard.

By now I guessed it was about ten o'clock. I waited for the glaring light in my cell to go off so I could get some sleep. While I waited I tried to calm myself. My nerves were on edge, mostly because I had no idea what was going to happen to me next. My life had suddenly turned into a roller-coaster ride in the dark. One moment I thought I was on my way to freedom, and the next I was convinced they were going to execute me. At times I even half expected a squad of Green Berets to burst into the jail and rescue me.

The night wore on, and still the light blazed in my cell. Every fifteen minutes or so I would hear footsteps stop outside my door, and then I would see eyes peering in through the hole at me.

I decided to sit against the wall on the opposite side so I would not be looking directly at the guard when he came to check on me. Instead, I sat staring at the sink and toilet.

Sometime around two o'clock in the morning I felt I had hit rock bottom. How much lower could things go for me? It was then that a shaft of hope hit me. Hadn't God told me I would have to go to the bottom before I got out? Then surely this was the *bottom*. And if I had to go to the *bottom* before I got out, then I was going to get out! I tried to focus on that thought as the night wore on.

I ended up not sleeping at all and was glad to hear the clanking breakfast trolley in the corridor soon after 3 A.M. It was Thursday morning, and as I waited for the trolley to get to my cell, I thought about what might happen today. Since the Muslim holy day was Friday, Thursday in Muslim countries was much like the first day of the week-end back in the United States. I wondered if I would be interrogated on a Thursday, or would they wait until Saturday?

Soon my cell door swung open, and the guard told me to stand in the center of the room with my plate. I held the plate out toward the doorway, and he dumped a large spoonful of rice onto it. He took the spoon and scraped some of the crisper browned rice from the side of the pot and put that on my plate as well. In Iran this browned, almost burned rice was considered a delicacy. The rice was topped off with a beef-and-pepper kebab, along with an orange and seven prunes. I was shocked, for compared to the food in the last place, this meal looked like a feast.

"The drink trolley will be along soon," the guard said as he shut the door.

I stood and waited, and sure enough, within a minute or two the door swung open again. I grabbed my mug and held it out too as the guard filled it with steaming hot tea. I took three sugar cubes from the plate he held out. However, I didn't drop them into my tea. I decided to save them to snack on when I got hungry during the day.

The morning dragged on. Of course there was no lunch, since it was Ramadan and everyone was supposed to be fasting during daylight hours. So around midday, I pulled out the sugar cubes and began to suck on them. But instead of satisfying my hunger, they made me feel sick.

I spent the whole day waiting tensely for something to happen, for a guard or an interrogator, even a lawyer, to appear in my cell. But it turned out to be a long and uneventful day, for which I was grateful.

That night, after sundown, a guard arrived at my door with dinner, which consisted of vegetable soup and tea. I sat down in the middle of my cell and ate it, all the while fantasizing about what it would be like to chomp into a seven-layer burrito at Taco Bell or a quarterpounder at McDonald's. I soon discovered that those kinds of fantasies didn't help the situation. They only made my present reality seem grimmer.

I was pretty sure that if they hadn't taken me to be interrogated on Thursday, they would not likely do it on Friday, a holy day.

Throughout Thursday and Friday, regular calls to prayer boomed throughout the prison over the loudspeaker system. On Friday afternoon, they played a long sermon. I could understand about half of what was being said, and what I understood upset me. The Muslim cleric spewed nothing but liturgies of hate and revenge. Over and over I heard the words "Death to America," "Death to Israel," "Death to Iraq," and "America is the great Satan." Even though I had been in and out of Muslim countries for years, I was still shocked by the vehemence of the accusations. If it was intended to intimidate me, it worked, for the fear I had been battling strengthened its grip on my mind.

About halfway through his tirade, the mullah said something about how we prisoners were in *Evin Prison* to help us become good Muslim citizens.

My blood ran cold. I was being held in Evin Prison! Evin was the most infamous prison in all of Iran. It was reserved for the most dangerous political prisoners. I shut my eyes and tried to clear my head. Did being in Evin Prison mean I was considered dangerous? Did it mean I would be incarcerated there for a long time? Had I been charged with some political crime? The questions took me in anxious circles and spiraled me down into despair. I had no answers to them.

I spent the next five hours pacing up and down in my cell worrying. One, two, three, four steps to the door, and four steps back to the corner. When I wasn't pacing, I sat with my back against the heater, staring at the door. Every hour or so throughout the day, a guard came to the window and stared in at me. If I didn't look attentive enough to the propaganda playing over the loudspeaker, he would yell at me until I showed suitable interest. I soon learned to perk up and pretend I was listening attentively whenever the guards came near my door.

Despite the hourly checkups, by sundown I was beginning to relax a little and think about the evening meal, relieved to have survived my first two days in Evin Prison.

TWELVE

Let the Games Begin

T H E following morning I decided I had to do something to try to keep my sanity. It was time to get out the *Beasleys* and the *Fat Fours.* These were two teams who had lived in my imagination since I was about seven years old. As a child I used to shoot baskets alone in the hoop over the garage door. To make the game more interesting, I developed two imaginary teams who played against each other. For a reason I have long since forgotten, I had named the teams the Beasleys and the Fat Fours.

Over the years I had become more creative, and the two teams were now much more defined in my head. Each team consisted of ten players, and I knew each of them by name and by the particular athletic traits they possessed. For example, number four player on the Fat Fours team was an old-timer, but he could still sparkle and pull off an incredible play if the team had its back to the wall. The number six players on both teams were the underdogs. They were the worst players on the team, and in tight situations, they often blew golden opportunities to put their team ahead. Meanwhile, the number eight player on each team was the power player. These players were capable of performing amazing athletic feats. Unfortunately, they were also overconfident. Instead of making some brilliant athletic move that could push their team ahead, they could just as easily blow the opportunity and put their team at a disadvantage. That was why I had to be careful when and where I used the number eight players in a game.

The Beasleys and the Fat Fours had added a competitive edge to the many games I had played alone as a child. They had been opponents in basketball, baseball, and tennis. And now I had called them up from my imagination so they could once again face each other in competition. Before we could start, though, I needed a ball of some sort and a game we could play with it. I looked around the cell to see what I could use for a ball. I could roll up the towel, but there was nothing to tie it with and stop it from unraveling as we played. I needed something with elastic in it that would pull tight and keep its shape.

In the end, I decided my underwear would be the best choice. Sure enough, if I rolled them up tightly with the elastic waistband on the outside, they made a firm ball. Once I had my ball ready, it was time for the games to begin.

After a few tries, "underwear bowling" became a big hit to help pass the time. I would sit with my back against the heating radiator, and the two teams would take turns bowling the "ball" along the tattered carpet. The object of the game was to get the ball as close as possible to the edge of the carpet without it going over. Going over the edge was an automatic default.

The Fat Fours, who were normally the underdogs, went first, followed by the Beasleys. The teams went up against each other two players at a time. Each set consisted of ten bowls, and I would mark off the ball's positions with pieces ripped from the empty cigarette packs I had found in the trash can in my cell. The underwear ball had to be rewrapped every two or three bowls as the game moved along.

Once all the players had taken a turn, I picked the top five players from each team to participate in a play-off game. At the end of the play-off game, I would announce the winning team, and the losing team would congratulate them.

I would concentrate so closely on the game, remembering who had what score and whose turn it was next, that an hour or two could easily slip by without my thinking about the prison walls that surrounded me.

When I got tired of bowling, the Beasleys and the Fat Fours would shoot hoops for a while. For this game I used pits from the prunes that were served with almost every meal. The objective of the game was to see who could land the most pits in the trash can.

I played these games for long periods of time, though I was never quite sure how long. In fact, not knowing how fast time was passing began to frustrate me after a while. I challenged myself to develop a method so I would know what time of day it was. On my second day in the cell, I noticed the bars on the window above the door made a shadow on the opposite wall. As soon as the shadow appeared in the morning, I banged on the door until a guard came. I asked him the time, and he told me it was nine o'clock. From then on, whenever I saw the shadow appear I knew it was nine o'clock. Over the next few days, I asked the guards what time it was at various intervals. Each time I put marks on the wall until I had a makeshift sundial that gave me a fairly accurate idea of what time it was until three-thirty in the afternoon, when the sun disappeared from my cell window.

On my fourth day in Evin Prison, at four-thirty in the afternoon, to my surprise and delight, a guard appeared in the cell door holding my Bible. I thought back to my arrival at the prison and how I had asked the guard with the kind face if I could keep my Bible with me. At the time I thought he hadn't cared, but it seemed he had reconsidered my request. I grabbed my Bible and held it close to my chest as the guard locked the door behind him. After he had gone, I flipped it open to the book of Matthew and began to read. In the coming weeks, my Bible would become a major source of comfort to me.

I couldn't hear much through the walls of my cell, though I often heard water running through the pipes into the next cell. After a while it struck me that my neighbor used a lot of water in the sink. He was probably washing items of clothing, I thought. Besides the games I had invented, I decided it was another activity that could fill up part of my day. I wasn't too worried about keeping my clothes clean, so I began to think about what else I could wash. In the end, I settled on my hair. It was getting longer, and I didn't have a comb. As a result, my hair had become matted, and my scalp itched terribly.

Unfortunately, I soon found the soap made my scalp itch more than it had before, but there was nothing I could do about that. Washing my hair was something to do, and it quickly became part of my daily routine. My days were now filled with basketball competitions, Bible reading, prayer, hair washing, eating, and the interminable wait to find out what would happen to me next.

Finally, on Wednesday, January 22, my eleventh day of incarceration, a guard came for me. He told me to pick up my towel and soap and then to put on my blindfold. He led me out of my cell and along an unfamiliar route. When I finally took off my blindfold, I found myself standing in a locker room. To my left was a shower, and not just any sort of shower, but one with American plumbing.

The guard pointed to a large cart piled with clothes. "Pick a clean set to wear," he ordered.

I rifled through the pants and tops looking for the biggest ones I could find. None were very large, but after a minute or two, I managed to find a pair of pants and a top I thought would almost fit me.

"Okay," the guard said, taking the new clothes from me, "get in the shower."

I stripped off my old prison pajamas as fast as I could in case there was a time limit on this excursion from my cell. With my dirty clothes lying in a pile on the floor, I stepped into the shower. The showerhead was mounted on the ceiling rather than the wall, and when I turned the faucet on, hot water cascaded down on me. I had never felt anything so good! I was fairly sure the shower was not bugged, so I sang my heart out as the soothing water streamed over me. For a minute or two, I almost forgot where I was. I kept waiting for the guard to tell me to get out, but he was leaning against the wall and didn't look in any hurry to get back on duty.

I stayed in the shower for over half an hour, and by the time I turned the water off, my skin was beginning to shrivel up. When I returned to my cell, not only was my skin clean and I was wearing fresh prison pajamas, but I also had a bounce in my step. Somehow the simple luxury of a shower had revived my spirits considerably.

On Friday morning, the guards came and got me from my cell. They escorted me down the corridor to what I thought was another prison cell. Instead, it was an empty mop closet. The biggest difference between my cell and the closet was that the closet had no ceiling. Overhead was a metal grid that opened to the sky. It felt amazing to breathe fresh air and to be able to see outside.

Unfortunately, after ten minutes the guard came back. "Time to go back," he said.

Reluctantly, I left the closet, but from then on, each Friday I was taken back to the mop closet for a short time. The guards referred to it as "fresh-air time."

The next day a guard opened the door to my cell and asked if I wanted to see a doctor.

"Yes," I replied, glad for any kind of distraction. I slipped on my blindfold loosely and waited to be led away. I was taken to the same administrative area where Glenn and I had been processed when we first arrived at Evin prison.

"Face the wall and wait," the guard said, leaving me standing beside several other men.

I peeked out of the side of my blindfold. On the wall to the right of me, I saw a painting of some snow-clad mountains. I didn't remember the picture from my first visit to this room, but the mountains reminded me of the Rockies and home. I spent a long time squinting to study the picture. It was the most beautiful sight I had seen in two weeks.

"Come," a guard said, leading me toward a desk. When we had come to a halt in front of it, he said, "Take off your blindfold now."

I did as instructed and discovered I was standing in front of a young man in a doctor's coat. He appeared to be about my age.

"You can speak to me in English," the doctor said in a British accent. "What seems to be your problem?"

"Well," I began, wondering how many times a day he heard the same complaint, "I can't sleep at night, and I'm depressed a lot of the time, especially when I get interrogated."

The doctor nodded his head as I spoke. "How much sleep are you getting?" he asked.

I thought for a moment. "I suppose about two or three hours over a twenty-four-hour period," I said.

His eyebrows rose. He thought for a long moment and then made his diagnosis. "Sir," he began, "I think you are suffering from anxiety and depression."

I wanted to say, "No kidding! You went to medical school for goodness knows how many years to figure that out?" Instead, I just nodded seriously.

"I can give you medicine to help," the doctor said. "It will be delivered to you later this evening. You are to take two pills before bedtime."

I thanked the doctor, pulled my blindfold on, and was escorted back to my cell.

Later that night, a bottle of Diazepam pills arrived for me from the pharmacy. Of course, the bottle had to stay on the shelf outside my door. When I was ready to try to get some sleep, I banged on the cell door and asked the guard for two of the pills.

It was such a relief to know I was finally going to get a good night's rest. I was a little worried, though, that I might possibly become addicted to the pills if I took them too often. However, I decided not to think about that too much, especially when they helped me to sleep deeply for four or five hours each night. Sometimes, I even awoke the next morning feeling refreshed.

During those days, I spent a lot of time reading my Bible. But no matter how much I read, it didn't seem to lift my spirits. I felt dead inside. Every morning I told myself God was there with me and that He loved me, but I sure didn't seem to be experiencing it.

Two days after the visit to the doctor, the cell door swung open for me to receive my food, and there waiting to serve me stood the second-highest official in the prison. I had no idea why he was manning the food cart that evening, but I obediently held out my plate to be filled with rice and gray-brown runny stew. After the official had filled my plate, I said, "Khali Mamnun," which as far as I knew was the Persian way to thank an important person who had done something for you.

I soon learned that those two words had sent shockwaves throughout the entire prison. The guards said to each other, "Can you believe that foreigner? He said 'Khali Mamnun' to the boss. Doesn't he know *anything* about Islamic law? That foreigner is a sinner, yet he dared to bless a devout Muslim!"

"I bet he gets five more months for saying that!" I overheard one guard say.

"Only five months?" another guard responded. "He'll get seven months at least."

As best I could figure out, I had said thank you in a particular form that also conveyed some sort of spiritual blessing upon the recipient— and not just any spiritual blessing, but one that implied equality with the person I was blessing.

Over the next five days, I overheard many of the guards repeatedly say that I would receive seven more months in prison because of what I had said. Although they could well have been playing games with me, I took what they said seriously and began to panic. In fact, during the daily Islamic radio broadcasts, the lyrics from some of the singers were about the foreigner getting seven more months for the mistake he had made. The entire prison knew what was going on with me.

I was shocked. Two simple words seemed to be turning my world upside down. And worse, there seemed to be no way to right the wrong I had done except to serve more prison time. I began to despair that I would be in Evin Prison for the rest of my life.

THIRTEEN

Day Fourteen

DAY fourteen proved to be the lowest point of my entire prison experience. The thought of having done something that could inadvertently lead to my spending seven more months in jail haunted me. I became even more pessimistic about ever being released. I began torturing myself with depressing thoughts: I'm an American in a country where the United States is referred to as the "Great Satan." Who am I kidding? They're never going to let me go. I've already been in prison for over two weeks, and I still haven't had a court hearing. I don't even know what I've been formally charged with.

As I sat in the corner mulling over these thoughts and feelings, I heard a voice inside my head say, "Come on home, Dan. Everything will be okay, just come on home." I recognized the voice as that of a friend from home who had died a year before. Then a second voice spoke into my mind. "Yeah, Dan, come on up. You'll love it here." This time it was the voice of my best friend from college. He had died at twenty-nine after getting sick on a mission trip to Africa.

I looked around the cell with one thought on my mind: How could I go to them? The only way I could join them was through death. Within a few moments, I was convinced God had allowed my friends to talk to me so that I would not be afraid to kill myself. However, committing suicide wouldn't be easy. The guards had made sure there was nothing sharp in my cell. Even my toothbrush was kept in the basket on the shelf outside my door, and it was only given to me under supervision. Figuring out a way to end my own life by outwitting the prison system so I could join my friends in heaven became a challenge for me.

My eyes soon rested on the sink on the far wall. Water! Surely I could drown myself in a sink full of water! As I thought about it, I realized I'd have to come up with a way to keep my head under water, even against my will. I studied the sink, as I had done so many times before. This time, though, I studied it with the eye of an engineer. It was secured to the wall on both sides with brackets. Suddenly, in a bolt of inspiration, the perfect plan came to me. If I plugged the sink with my shirt, it would fill up. Then I could tie one end of my towel to the left bracket and the other end loosely around the right bracket. Once I put my head into the water, I would pull the end of the towel into a tight knot that I could not untie even if I wanted to. In fact, if my plan worked, any struggling on my part would only tighten the towel that much more, making it impossible for me to escape. Within a minute or so, my lungs would be filled with water, and I would be in heaven with my friends.

With the "invitation" from my two friends still ringing in my ears, I tied one end of the towel to the bracket and waited for the guard to do his rounds and check on me. As soon as he had passed my cell, I completed my preparations and got ready to follow through with my plan. With any luck, the next time the guard checked on me, my life would have long since departed from this prison cell.

I pulled off my pajama jacket and plugged the sink. I filled it with water and stuck my head under for a couple of short pre-runs. The sensation of gasping for air was a horrible one, but I told myself it was the price I had to pay to free myself from this life and escape into the next.

I took the loose end of the towel and wrapped it around the right bracket twice. Without thinking about it or trying to draw one last deep gasp of air, I plunged my head into the sink. The water was cold against my face as I reached for the end of the towel. I pulled on it, stretching it out and forcing my head farther down into the sink. As I prepared to loop the towel around the bracket one last time to knot it firmly in place, my hands began to tremble violently. I tried to keep going, but the urge inside to release the tension on the towel and pull my head out and breathe deeply was too strong. Before I could get the feeling in check, I had released the towel and lifted my head out of the water.

I collapsed onto the floor, gasping for air. Twenty minutes passed before I finally stopped coughing up water and began breathing normally again. While I was disappointed my suicide attempt had failed, I knew the system I had rigged up would work. I promised myself my next try wouldn't fail. Next time I would not allow my hands to shake or my resolve to waver. I would pull the knot tight. There would be no turning back. I comforted myself with the thought that I was only minutes away from eternity.

I clambered to my feet and checked that the towel was still secured to the bracket at both ends and then topped off the sink with more water. I thought of my college friend's words as I thrust my head into the water one last time. I reached for the end of the towel, determined to go all the way this time. I was just about to pull the knot tight and trap my head under the water when something broke inside me. Once again I released the tension on the towel and collapsed to the floor. My body racked with deep, uncontrollable sobs. I lay on the thin carpet crying for a long time before it became clear to me what I had almost succeeded in doing. The thoughts I had had were not from my deceased friends. I was devastated to think I had almost obeyed them. Deep in my heart I knew my attempt at suicide had been wrong.

I thought back to my thirty-third birthday party the previous December 14. At the party several friends had said to me, "Dan, Jesus died when he was thirty-three, you know." I knew they meant it as a joke, but somehow the thought had lodged itself deep in my mind. It felt like a warning, perhaps a premonition that Satan was going to try to take my life sometime during that year. And here I was helping him out! I had known since I was a young boy that the Bible says Satan disguises himself as an angel of light. I realized it was he who had tricked me into thinking my friends wanted me to commit suicide in order to join them. The thought shocked me. Satan had nearly succeeded in gaining the ultimate victory over me. I had almost destroyed myself.

I sat stunned at how close I had come to throwing my life away. Guilt and remorse washed over me in waves, and I began to cry out to God. "Please forgive me, God. I give myself back to you," I prayed. "The only place I am safe is in your presence. I will stay in prison the rest of my life if that is where you want me. But I promise, no matter what happens, I will never try to kill myself again. I know it's not the way you have for me to get out of this place. I will walk the path you have made for me and not try to make my own way. Amen."

Following the suicide attempt, I felt a closeness with God that I had not experienced in prison up until this time. I had a new joy and certainty in my heart. And I sensed a new expectation inside that I couldn't explain. I had a deep conviction that something significant was going to happen the next day. Somehow I knew God was going to say something important to me then.

By 7 A.M. the next day, I was so excited I could barely stand it. However, I made myself follow my usual morning routine. I read two psalms at seven and waited until about eight before I picked up my Bible again. Before I began reading, I prayed. "God, I know you are here with me, and I sense that you have something special to say this morning. Please guide me now." I opened my eyes, sure God was about to speak to me.

I randomly opened my Bible and, looking down, saw it was opened at the Old Testament book of Daniel, chapter ten. My eyes fell on verses twelve and thirteen. I read them expectantly. "Then he continued, 'Do not be afraid, Daniel. Since the first day that you set your mind to gain understanding and to humble yourself before your God, your words were heard, and I have come in response to them. But the prince of the Persian kingdom resisted me twenty-one days. Then Michael, one of the chief princes, came to help me, because I was detained there with the king of Persia."

I scooted back and leaned against the wall, hardly able to take in what I had just read. I had never before felt such a powerful sense that God was speaking to me through Scripture as I felt at that moment. I read the passage again. "Do not be afraid, Daniel." Okay, I told myself, I am not to be afraid anymore. "Since the first day that you set your mind to gain understanding and to humble yourself before your God, your words were heard, and I have come in response to them." God had been with me the whole time, watching over me. "But the prince of the Persian kingdom resisted me twenty-one days." Wow! I got goose bumps as I reread those words. It had been exactly twenty-one days since my passport had been taken from me at the border. Now I was in prison, and not just any prison, but a high-security prison in the heart of the Persian kingdom.

I read on and became even more excited when I got to verse nineteen. "'Do not be afraid, O man highly esteemed,' he said. 'Peace! Be strong now; be strong.'"

The word *peace* resonated within me. For the first time since I'd been arrested, I knew everything was going to work out. A voice inside said, "You will get out in my way, and in my time." I also knew beyond a shadow of doubt that God had allowed me to be in prison for a purpose. I was in His hands. Even though I couldn't see the bigger picture, He could, and I intended to trust Him totally from that moment on.

Throughout the rest of the day, I reread that passage many times, and with each reading, hope welled within me. I was exactly where God wanted me to be. It might feel as though I were in the pit of hell, but I was not there by accident. I was there because God had a definite plan for me to be there, whether I understood it or not.

This revelation released an even greater love for those around me, especially the other prisoners. Almost every night I heard someone being whipped or beaten, and I came to identify the sudden piercing cry of a man when electrodes were attached to his toes and high voltage was shot through his body. I began to compare my situation to that of the other prisoners. Even though I'd had no contact with the outside world, at least the South African embassy knew I had last been seen inside an Iranian government building. And I was sure that by now the Swiss and American governments would be working on my behalf. I also knew my parents and home church would have mobilized, too, and that many people would be praying for me and writing letters to secure my release. But most of the other prisoners had no one outside of Iran who even knew they existed. Their human rights were being violated brutally and trampled on each day, and no one was petitioning for them or praying for their release. What was worse, despite what happened to me, I knew I was safe in Jesus' arms for eternity, while these Iranian prisoners had nothing to hope in. They had nothing to bring meaning to the hell they were living through.

I thought, too, of Glenn. I was sure he had been released by now, because the guards no longer mentioned him in their gossip sessions. He had been delivered from the hell of Evin Prison, while most of the other prisoners would probably never taste such freedom again. They faced an uncertain future, not knowing if each new day that dawned would be their last.

Yet despite this grim reality, the more I prayed, the more hope welled up within me that God had a specific purpose for my being in Evin Prison. And I knew that somehow I would soon discover what that purpose was.

FOURTEEN

"How Do You Plead?"

THE conviction that God had a special purpose for me being in Evin Prison did not fade, though nothing on the outside seemed to change. The guards continued to spend their idle hours standing at the end of the corridor gossiping about me. The tiniest things I did were reported to the group and discussed as if I were a zoo specimen. They even discussed the fact that I swallowed my orange seeds instead of spitting them out. What was worse, there was nothing I could do to tune out the noise of their discussions. Nor could I stop the guards from peering in at me whenever they liked, even when I was using the toilet. I began to get a little paranoid. After a while I wished that I didn't understand Persian. That way the guards' daily discussions would be nothing but garbled noise to me.

From some of the comments the guards made, I came to the conclusion there must be a hidden microphone somewhere in my cell. It was probably in the ceiling. Knowing that I was being listened to made it difficult to think of praying or singing out loud. I couldn't help but wonder if I would hear my words mocked later in the day. I found myself wanting to talk aloud less and less. By about my thirty-fifth day of incarceration, I had decided to remain silent as much as possible.

After being left alone in my cell and studied through the peephole in the door for so long, I was surprised when on Tuesday, February 18, two guards opened the door and marched into my cell. "Let's go!" ordered the older of the two men.

I scrambled to my feet and reached for my blindfold. I wondered as they led me along if I was going to be interrogated again. Instead of walking toward the stairs that led to the interrogation rooms, however, I was taken in the opposite direction, toward the front entrance of the prison.

"Sit down and wait here," a guard snapped when we reached a worn wooden bench outside an office.

I did as I was told and waited as the minutes ticked by. Finally, I heard two sets of footsteps at the far end of the corridor. I turned my head sideways so I could see out the side of my blindfold who it was. To my shock, I saw Glenn walking alongside a guard. My mind could scarcely take it in. I had been so certain that Glenn had been released from prison days, maybe even weeks, before. But now here he was, like an apparition from the past.

"You're still here?" I blurted.

"Yeah, I'm here," Glenn said flatly as he sat down beside me.

My mind went blank for a moment. I couldn't think of anything else to say to my friend. Slowly, as I sat staring at him through the corner of my blindfold, I began to take in the details. Unlike me, Glenn was not blindfolded, and he was wearing his street clothes. "Do you know what's happening?" I finally whispered.

"I'm not sure," Glenn replied, "but I think they're taking us to the courthouse."

"You do?" I said.

"Yes," Glenn said. "I was there yesterday. They loaded about fifteen of us up and took us to the courthouse."

"What did you do there?" I asked.

"Well, I waited for a long time, but in the end I got to see a judge.

He asked me a few general questions and then sent me to the bus to be transported back here."

"So what's going to happen now?" I asked, aware that Glenn probably had no more real information than I did.

"I don't know," he said. "I hope we get out, but it's been a mighty time here in prison, eh? God has been so good to me."

"Yeah," I said, studying Glenn's clear eyes and calm smile. "I guess you have been sleeping okay at night, too?"

"Like a baby," he said. "They let me have your Bible for about two weeks, and I meditated on Philippians, especially chapter four, verse eight, which talks about thinking only on things that are true. It's been a challenge. I've been trying to put it into practice and take every thought captive. It's been really great."

For a brief moment, I envied Glenn. Throughout our trip, he had been able to sleep soundly at night, while I lay awake rehashing the events of each day and imagining what difficulties and dangers might lie ahead. Now, in prison, even with my pills, I was only sleeping for about four hours a night, while Glenn looked well rested. "Well, you've been doing better than me," I finally confessed. "Half the time I think I'm going to crack up."

Glenn reached over and put his hand on my arm. "It's going to be okay, Dan," he said. "We have to trust God. I know it will turn out all right, eh?"

"Yeah, I know," I replied. "But pray for me. It's not easy holding on, and I don't want my mind to crack."

I shut my eyes, thinking of my attempted suicide. I didn't have time to explain it to Glenn right then. I wondered if he had any idea of how close I'd come to the ultimate breakdown.

"Stand up," commanded a guard who had walked up beside us.

Glenn and I stood and followed along as we were led outside.

Once outside, to my amazement, I was told I could take off my blindfold. I pulled it off and looked around. It was about ten o'clock in the morning, and it was a sunny winter day. The white blanket of snow that covered the ground was such a stark contrast to the dingy prison. I took a deep breath of the air that smelled so fresh. For the first time

I could see clearly where I was. I was standing in a driveway with a cream-colored brick building behind me and a fifteen-foot-high wall in front of me. To my left a number of other prisoners were standing by an old Mercedes minibus. I did a quick head count and counted nineteen of us in all.

Finally, the guard gave a nod, and the prisoners began boarding the bus. They acted as if this was a common occurrence for them. Glenn and I followed right along behind, and soon we were all packed into the vehicle. Glenn and I sat in the third row from the front on the right-hand side.

I didn't much care where the bus took me as the driver shoved it into gear and headed toward the front gate. Just to be outside was such an unexpected treat. I had my blindfold off, and I was traveling away from Evin Prison. Whatever happened, after thirty-eight days of being cooped up all alone in a cell, I was finally going to see the countryside again.

After our names were checked against a master list at the front checkpoint, the metal gates were swung open, and we drove out and away from Evin.

Only one guard was on the bus. Although he had made an announcement telling us no one was allowed to talk on the journey, everyone was whispering to one another. I could even hear the occasional eruption of laughter.

Leaving Evin Prison behind, we headed south toward downtown Tehran. I was torn between wanting to catch up on all that had happened to Glenn and wanting to stare out the bus window and take in the beauty of nature. After all I had been through, I could hardly comprehend that people out there were going about their normal daily routines. Women carrying huge bags of vegetables walked along the street, and men driving cars passed the bus. I wondered if I would ever drive a car again, or walk carefree along the street, or go into a store with money in my pocket and decide for myself what I wanted to buy. All those everyday choices I had taken for granted for years had now been stripped away, and everything I could or could not do was decided for me by others. It felt bittersweet seeing regular life from the vantage point of a spectator rather than a participant.

I thought back to a day when I was about twelve years old. My father was driving me down the 110 freeway toward Los Angeles, and a prison bus was in front of us. As we passed the bus, I remember looking in and seeing the men in their prison uniforms. I wondered how a man could ever let himself sink so low as to end up being a prisoner. I decided the prisoners riding in that bus could be nothing but losers. Now I was the prisoner in the bus looking out at all of the young kids who stared as we drove by. This time I felt like a loser.

As we approached downtown, the traffic got more congested. Glenn told me we were following the same route as the day before, which made it increasingly likely that we were indeed headed for the courthouse. After about twenty minutes of rolling along, the bus pulled up in front of a large compound, and we were ordered to get out.

Outside, we were told to stay in a group as we walked across the parking lot and into a large stone building. Once inside, we marched up the stairs to the third floor. As we walked through the building, I noticed many small offices lining each side of the corridor. Finally, a guard pointed to a long, well-worn wooden bench and told us all to sit down. I chose a spot near a filing cabinet and plopped down to begin the waiting game.

"This is where I was yesterday," Glenn whispered. "A man came out of that door and called me in to see a judge."

"Then what happened?" I asked.

"Not much, eh?" Glenn said. "Like I said, the judge asked me a few questions about what I was doing in Iran, and then I was sent back to the bus."

"Were you wearing your prison uniform?" I asked.

"Yeah," he replied. "They only gave me my clothes back this morning. I'm so glad to be wearing something that fits me again, eh."

"What do you think it means?" I asked, trying not to get my hopes up.

"Well, they told me I was going to be released today, but I'm not sure if that's true or not."

Yesterday was the first time Glenn had been taken to the courthouse, and today he was most likely going to be set free. What did it mean for me? Was I following the same pattern, only a day later? I had no way of knowing. Glenn's potential release could represent a good thing or a bad thing for my situation.

All evidence indicated that I had reason to hope my freedom might be close at hand, but I still had some doubts, which I finally voiced to Glenn. "Well, if you're leaving, that means the South African government must have struck a bargain to get you out, but the Iranian government and the United States are never going to work out a deal for me. I could be locked up here for life."

"No!" Glenn said, trying to encourage me. "You're going to make it."

I thought for a moment about all the simple freedoms Glenn would have in a few hours. He would be free to talk to his family. "You've got to call my mom and say hi from me," I finally said. "The form I filled in at the South African embassy has her name and number on it. I bet you can't wait to talk to your family. It's one of the things I miss the most," I added.

Glenn frowned for a moment. "What do you mean? You get to call home every couple of weeks, don't you?"

"No," I replied, astonished by his question. "Do you get to make phone calls?"

"Yes, I've made two, both to South Africa," Glenn said. "And the embassy meetings? They let you meet with the Swiss embassy staff, don't they?"

"No," I blurted. "I haven't talked to a soul."

"You're kidding!" Glenn said, surprise and concern evident in his voice.

I couldn't believe it. Why hadn't I been given the same privileges? We were being treated so differently that any hope I had of following Glenn out of prison the following day evaporated instantly.

"What did the embassy staff say to you?" I asked when I had gathered my composure.

Just as Glenn was about to reply, a guard stepped into the room. "Glenn Murray," he said, looking at a sheet of paper he was holding.

Glenn and I both stood up. I hugged him tightly, sure I would not see him again for a very long time.

"I'll do all I can for you when I get out, and I promise to not stop praying until you're out of here," he whispered, and then he followed the guard out through the door.

My eyes blurred with tears as I realized Glenn was gone. Now I was really alone.

Thankfully, the guard reappeared a minute later and announced it was time for a bathroom break. Getting up and walking around would help take my mind off of saying good-bye to Glenn.

I followed the other prisoners down the hall and into a long bathroom. The first thing I noticed was the bars across the window, and the second was the mirror that ran along behind the washbasins. I approached it with some trepidation. I had not seen myself for five and a half weeks and didn't know what to expect. I knew my hair was long and matted, but knowing that did not prepare me for what I saw. As I looked into the mirror, a Robinson Crusoe-like figure with a beard and bloodshot eyes stared back at me. I pulled up my prison shirt. Each of my ribs stuck out.

I stood for a long time in front of the mirror until I realized all the other prisoners were looking at me as they squatted on their haunches against the far wall, puffing on cigarettes. I pulled down my shirt and splashed some cold water on my face. As I did so they began peppering me with questions: Who are you? Why are you here? What did you do to end up in Evin Prison?

I felt confused. I wondered whether or not I should answer their questions. What if one of them was a government spy planted there to see what I would say? How could I trust these people? As my confusion began to turn to panic, I shook my head, unwilling to say anything that might get me in more trouble.

After a while we all drifted back to our places on the wooden bench, and I sat silently waiting to be called before the judge.

Eventually, though, I let down my guard enough to talk to the prisoner sitting next to me. He appeared to be an old hand at these court visits, and I believed what he told me. He said every prisoner in Evin was given the opportunity at least once a month to see a judge regarding his or her case. I couldn't imagine how such frequent court visits benefited most of the prisoners, but at least it gave them a "day out."

I noticed that many of the other prisoners appeared to be good friends and laughed and joked among themselves. I envied their closeness and obvious camaraderie and asked my neighbor about it. He told me the men got to know one another so well because they lived together in bunkrooms back at Evin. Indeed, the prison had many bunkrooms. Only the most dangerous prisoners were kept in solitary confinement as I was.

The man also told me there were ways inside the prison to get certain supplies. He asked if I needed anything. I looked down at my socks. They had huge holes in the bottoms from my constant pacing. "Socks would be great," I said, wondering why a stranger would take the time to be kind to me.

The man patted me on the back and smiled. "The next time I see you, I will have new socks for you. Just you wait and see," he said encouragingly.

I smiled back, hoping I was on my way home and that there would not be a next time. The last thing I wanted to do was get back on that bus and return to the prison.

The clock on the wall said 12:30 as I finally followed a guard out the door. We walked along a short hallway and then turned left into a large room. It looked much like an American courtroom, with a long, polished wooden table across the front. Beyond it was another, shorter table, where I presumed the judge would sit. Among the people in the room, I recognized my interrogator, Mr. Akram, and a younger man who had been the official interpreter when Glenn and I were first detained weeks before.

The guard motioned for me to sit at one end of the long table. As I sat down I surveyed the room some more. I was surprised by how "high-tech" it was. Cords and cables crisscrossed the floor, linking television monitors to video cameras.

Twenty minutes passed before we were all asked to rise when the judge entered the room. He looked to be about thirty-five or forty years old, and he wore a crisp white shirt with no tie, as was the custom of upper-class Iranian men. He told us to be seated, and I watched as the cameraman stepped forward and began to videotape the proceedings.

"*The State* versus *Mr. Daniel Baumann.* How do you plead?" the judge asked.

My mouth went dry. This was not some informal meeting. I suddenly realized I was on trial! I didn't know what I had been formally accused of, I had no legal counsel, and it was my turn to speak. I supposed I should plead not guilty, but to what? I felt as though I were stuck in a bad dream. "Jesus," I prayed, "you told your disciples not to be afraid when they were dragged before rulers. You said the Holy Spirit would give us the words to speak. Help me now to know what to say."

The judge's voice cut through my prayer. "Mr. Baumann, do you work for the United States Secret Service?"

Even though I understood the judge's words, I was grateful to have the interpreter tell me what he had said in English. A courtroom was the worst place in which to make a linguistic mistake like the one I had made back at Evin Prison. "No, sir, I do not," I replied in English.

My answer was relayed back through the interpreter to the judge.

"Then can you tell us exactly why you came to Iran?"

"Yes, sir, I can," I said. "I came into Iran as a tourist. I entered on a tourist visa."

The interpreter busily relayed my words in Farsi.

"But what was the main reason you came, Mr. Baumann?" the judge asked.

I took a deep breath. It was now or never. I shot another silent prayer toward heaven asking for wisdom and then began to speak. "The main reason I've come to Iran is because I am a Christian, and I want to find ways in which I can tell Iranian people about Jesus Christ."

I watched the judge's eyebrows rise.

"And why did you feel that was necessary, Mr. Baumann?"

"Because I believe He can change anyone's life and give them a reason for living."

I felt sure that saying something that bold would only inflame the situation, but I wanted to have my testimony on record. That way if I was hanging on the gallows and someone wanted to know what I had been killed for, they could review the tape and know I had died for a purpose. If I was going to be a martyr, I wanted it to be for the right reason: that I had spoken the truth about my faith in the Lord.

The judge continued asking me about my Christian beliefs, and as he did, I felt a godly confidence building within me. The more I spoke the truth, the bolder I felt.

A few minutes later, the judge pulled out an envelope and handed it to a guard with instructions to pass it to me. I unfolded the top of the envelope, and inside was a stack of photographs.

"Go ahead, look at them, Mr. Baumann," the judge said. "I have some questions to ask you about them."

It took me a few seconds to flick through the photographs, and as I did, I actually felt sick with worry. They were not my photos. They were from Glenn's camera, and they showed the faces of many of the friends we had made during our stay in Iran, both Christian and Muslim. I cringed, not for my sake, but for theirs, especially when I noticed that a young woman in one of the photos was holding a Bible in her hand.

The judge asked me many questions about the photos, and I answered as best I could, though I could not remember all the details relating to some of the pictures.

Two hours into the questioning, the judge announced we would recess for a short break. I used the opportunity to go to the bathroom and take a few deep breaths.

While I waited for the judge to return, the interpreter came up to me, his face contorted into a leering smile. "The cameraman wants to get saved," he sneered. "Why don't you tell him how to do it?"

"Maybe we could talk about it later. Now is not the right time," I responded as calmly as I could to his taunting.

The exchange, short as it was, worried me. This hostile interpreter was responsible to convey my answers accurately to the judge. And although I understood most of what he said, I knew he could slant my answers in ways that I would not pick up on, such as being overly sarcastic or disrespectful. I prayed hard, asking God to help me to stay calm while this young man translated my words.

After the break, the line of questioning changed as the judge began to ask about my time in prison. He wanted to know if I was being fed regularly, and if I had been abused in any way.

I answered as honestly as I could.

The judge then asked me if I had any questions.

"Yes, Your Honor, I do," I said, thinking of Glenn. "I would like to know when I will be able to talk to someone from the Swiss embassy."

The judge looked puzzled for a moment and then abruptly changed tack, asking me more questions about why I had come to Iran.

Finally, at around four o'clock, the video camera was turned off, and I was escorted from the courtroom to the room where I had last seen Glenn. I wondered if he was a free man by now. I had been wait-ing on the bench for about half an hour when the door opened and the judge walked in. I jumped to my feet.

"Tomorrow you will meet representatives from the Swiss embassy at Evin Prison," he said in perfectly accented English.

As he spoke, I thought I saw his lips curl into a slight smile.

"Thank you," I replied, excited that I was finally going to meet someone who would be on my side. I was also happy to know that the judge spoke such good English. Even though everything in the court-room had been channeled through the hostile interpreter, I knew the judge had understood most of what I'd said in English.

After the judge left, I was told the bus with the other prisoners had already left for Evin Prison. I would have to wait for paperwork to be processed so I could be driven back to the prison in a car. All this red tape took about an hour, and then I was escorted outside to a small green Toyota Corolla that was waiting beside the curb.

The driver, probably no older than twenty-five, sat in the car look-ing around nervously.

I waited as three other prisoners emerged from the building and were marched over to the car. As they approached, the driver clambered out. He pulled a pair of handcuffs from his back pocket and hand-cuffed me to the oldest prisoner of the group.

The other prisoners became angry and scolded the driver. "What did you do that for?" they demanded. "Let him go. You're crazy to handcuff him."

They seemed to think the driver was overreacting. I did, too. After thirty-eight days in prison, I was not in prime physical shape to make a run for it. The driver had clicked the handcuffs so tightly around our wrists that I felt sorry for the old man handcuffed to me.

Ignoring the complaints of the other prisoners, a guard motioned for us to get into the car. My handcuffed partner and I climbed awk-wardly into the backseat, he first and then I. For a brief moment, it was almost possible to believe I was a regular person out for a drive in the country. Unfortunately, my fantasy didn't last long. I couldn't stop thinking of what had just happened in that courtroom and the impli-cations of some of the questions asked me by the judge. Though no

formal charges had ever been made and an absolute lack of legal procedure surrounded the entire scenario, I knew they were trying to
falsely charge me with being a spy. A shiver of fear ran through me as
the Toyota pulled back through the main gate of Evin Prison, and once
again I was prisoner number fifty-eight.

FIFTEEN

Someone Was
on My Side

THE metal door swung shut behind me, and once again I
was alone in my cell. Dinner was waiting for me in the middle of the
floor. It looked like a blob of brown, pureed baby food, but I ate some
of it anyway, scooping up the mush with pieces of flatbread. As I ate my
meal, I thought about the events of the day. From what Glenn had said,
I had real hopes that I might finally be set free. I could hardly believe
what I had heard in the courtroom. *The State* versus *Mr. Daniel
Baumann*. I thought I was going to have the opportunity to present my
case of being wrongfully detained, and hoped for a release, and yet now
I had a serious foreboding from the line of questions the judge had
asked. Especially when he asked if I worked for the United States Secret
Service. He had seemed concerned, however, when he found out I had
not talked to anyone from the embassy. And I wanted to trust the
judge. When he said someone from the Swiss embassy would visit me
tomorrow, part of me took him at his word. I thought he seemed sincere when he said it. Yet another part of me said it was foolish to trust

anyone associated with the Iranian justice system. After all, I hadn't received much justice yet. Still, Glenn had been allowed to see someone from his embassy, so I did my best to hold on to the hope that officials from the Swiss embassy would come and visit me soon.

When I had eaten all the food I wanted, I flushed the rest down the toilet. After washing my bowl and cleaning off my tablecloth, I rapped on the door and asked the guard for my sleeping medication.

Even after taking the medication, I lay awake for hours, trying to decide what I should tell the Swiss authorities if they did come. By the time morning rolled around, my head was brimming with a list of questions: What was happening with my case? How long would I be locked up for? What was I being formally charged with? Did the American government know about my situation? What were they doing to help? Had my case been on TV in the United States? Did embassy officials know that I had been interrogated and beaten regularly?

Several days earlier, a guard had stormed into my cell, thrown several sheets of paper and a pencil at my feet, and told me to once again write a list of everything I had done since arriving in Iran. In hindsight, the list was probably in preparation for my appearance in court. When I had finished writing the list, the guard never asked me to give back the pencil or unused sheets of paper. I quickly ferreted them away under the edge of the carpet.

After breakfast, I slipped the paper and pencil out of their hiding place and began to scribble down all the questions I wanted to ask.

I had just finished jotting down the last question when the cell door burst open. "What are you writing?" a guard demanded as he stepped inside.

My heart started to pound, and I was frightened. I had been so preoccupied with getting my questions down on paper that I'd forgotten to keep a lookout for the guard and his prying eyes. "Nothing important," I replied, hurriedly folding the sheet of paper and stuffing it into my front pocket. The last thing I needed was their getting any information they could twist and use to incriminate me with more false charges.

The guard grunted and motioned for me to pick up my towel. A burst of hope surged through me. It was Wednesday, not Thursday, my regular shower day. Perhaps I was being taken to the shower to clean myself up before seeing someone from the Swiss embassy!

I reached out to grab my blindfold, but the guard stopped me. "Let me have that piece of paper first," he said.

I tried to think fast. The last thing I wanted was the prison authorities to know exactly what I was going to ask the Swiss officials. If they didn't like what was on the list, they could easily cancel any planned visit with embassy staff. "No," I said in a casual voice, wondering how far I dared try to resist his demand. "It's okay, you don't need it."

"Now," the guard snapped.

"Oh, come on," I cajoled, hoping he might give me a break. "It's nothing important, just a few private things I wrote down."

The guard stepped forward and reached for my pocket. I could see the veins on the side of his neck bulging in anger. I had no other choice, so I pulled the paper out and handed it over.

All the way to the shower, I chastised myself for being so stupid as to write something down. Had I just blown my chance at seeing someone from the Swiss embassy? I desperately hoped not.

The guard's mood did not improve while I was in the shower. Normally I could shower for as long as I liked, but this morning the guard reached in and turned the water off after only a couple of minutes. In silence I dried and changed into a new set of prison pajamas before putting on my blindfold and being led back to my cell. It was ten o'clock before the door opened again. This time, to my surprise, it was Mr. Akram standing there.

"Let's go," he said, smiling.

He seemed genuinely happy to see me, though I didn't trust him one bit. I put on my blindfold without thinking. The idea of walking around the prison without it was foreign to me now. I was led along the corridor that my cell opened off of, but at the end of it, instead of turning left as always, we went right. My heart began to beat wildly. Something different was definitely happening. I only hoped and prayed it was something good!

We walked on a few more yards, and then Mr. Akram said, "You can take off your blindfold now."

I pulled it off and looked around. We were walking through a set of double doors and out into the sunlight. "What's going to happen now?" I asked as I looked up and took in the vast expanse of the sky.

"I'm taking you to meet the Swiss authorities," he said pleasantly, and then his tone changed abruptly. He turned to face me. "Mr. Baumann, you must not say a word about the interrogation sessions. I will be there listening to you, and I will know everything you say. You must not say anything about how you have been treated in here. It is none of the Swiss's business. All they need to know is that you are fine and that you have been treated well. To say anything else would not be in your best interest. Do you understand what I am saying, Mr. Baumann?" Mr. Akram pointed at me to emphasize his last statement.

I nodded. I understood exactly what he was saying and the under- lying threat he was making. I had no doubt Mr. Akram already had the list of questions I was planning to ask. He was making sure I would not be allowed to be alone with the Swiss authorities. *So much for a private meeting*, I thought gloomily as we walked side by side along a concrete path.

We walked on in silence past a couple of chicken coops and a gar- den, which I guessed were part of a prison work program. After a few minutes, a single-story brick building came into view. Mr. Akram pointed at it.

"In there," he said cheerfully, all the menace of his previous com- ments gone from his voice.

We entered the building and turned right into a reception area.

"Stay here," Mr. Akram said, looking as nervous as I felt.

I waited silently as he disappeared into a side room. A few moments later he emerged. "Everything is ready," he announced, and then under his breath he added, "Remember what I told you. If you do not say what I told you to say, you will suffer the consequences."

I followed Mr. Akram into the adjoining room. At the end of a long mahogany table sat two neatly dressed European men. Both men rose when they saw me enter.

"It is good to see you, Mr. Baumann," said the older and taller of the two men in flawless English, shaking my hand vigorously. "I am David Steiner, chargé d'affaires with the Swiss embassy."

The other man, who was short and stocky and wore horn-rimmed glasses, introduced himself as Walter Graff, a consular official from the embassy. After the introductions, the men invited me to sit down at the table.

I sat down opposite the chargé d'affaires. I noticed he was clad in an expensive pinstriped business suit, while I had on striped prison pajamas. Despite my elation at meeting the two men, I suddenly felt extremely self-conscious about my unkempt appearance.

As Mr. Steiner pulled some papers from his briefcase, the door swung open and in walked the interpreter from the courthouse, along with two other official-looking Iranian men and a woman. They all took their places beside Mr. Akram at the long table, and the woman pulled a pad of paper from her bag.

I felt totally deflated. My dream of a private meeting with the Swiss officials was in ruins. As I wondered what I should say, I could still hear Mr. Akram's threat echoing in my mind.

"Let's get down to business," the chargé d'affaires said in a business-like voice.

The interpreter translated his words into Farsi for the others.

"Mr. Baumann, do you know what they have charged you with?" David Steiner asked.

"No, sir," I replied. "I have no idea." Though no formal charge had ever been mentioned, I realized they suspected me of working for the CIA, which would have serious consequences. But I didn't dare even mention it in this conversation.

"No idea?" he echoed, raising his eyebrows as he gave Mr. Akram a steely glare. "And how have you been treated in here?"

I felt my heart beat wildly. Should I defy Mr. Akram and tell the chargé d'affaires about my interrogation and the beatings? Would it help me or hurt me? I didn't know, but I remembered how I had committed myself to tell the truth to the Iranian authorities. As I sat there praying silently for wisdom, the thought struck me that the same standard ought to apply to the Swiss authorities as well. I took a deep breath and deliberately avoided looking in Mr. Akram's direction. "I have been subjected to many hours of interrogation," I said, "and some of it has not been good. Sometimes I have been hit and slapped by my interrogators."

The graying hair on Mr. Steiner's temples twitched, and his eyebrows rose as he listened to my words. I also heard Mr. Akram shift nervously in his chair.

The chargé d'affaires asked me more questions about the interrogation sessions, and I held nothing back. It was a relief to finally tell someone who cared about everything I'd had to endure in the last weeks. It was as if a great burden rolled off of me.

After a few minutes, I asked about my parents. "Are you in contact with my father and mother?"

David Steiner nodded. "They are very concerned about you, of course, and we keep in close contact. They told me to tell you many people are praying for you."

"Thank you," I said. "May I ask what the embassy's official position on my imprisonment is?"

The chargé d'affaires and the consular officer both sat up straight in their chairs. "I can assure you, Mr. Baumann, you have the total commitment of the Swiss government to get you out of prison. We have been offered no explanation as to why you are here. From our point of view, you are being illegally detained. We are very upset with the Iranian government for detaining you." Then, to underscore his point, David Steiner looked Mr. Akram directly in the eye and repeated, "We are *very upset* with the Iranian government for detaining you."

"Thank you," I said, relieved they were totally on my side.

"Have they allowed you your phone call yet?" This time the question came from Walter Graff.

"No," I said. "I haven't been allowed to phone anyone since I've been here."

"Well, that is a violation of your rights," he said. "You should have been. You are entitled to one ten-minute phone call every two weeks." Then turning to Mr. Akram, he added, "I expect to be informed when Mr. Baumann has made his phone call."

Adjusting his horn-rimmed glasses, Walter Graff then asked me, "Do you get one hour a week outside?"

"No. The only time I get to go outside is when I'm being taken somewhere, and once a week I get ten minutes in a mop closet that has no ceiling, just a metal grid open to the outside."

"That must be remedied, too," Walter Graff said pointedly, once again glaring at Mr. Akram.

David Steiner took up the questioning again. "Was it your choice to not have us visit you until now?" he asked.

I laughed incredulously. "I would have loved to have seen you on my first day here!" I exclaimed. "Unfortunately, I didn't know such a visit was permitted."

The chargé d'affaires's voice grew terse. "It is a requirement to inform all prisoners of their right to see a member from their embassy within two days of being detained." He turned to Mr. Akram and asked, "You never informed Mr. Baumann he had a right to contact his embassy?"

"He never asked to see you," my interrogator replied weakly.

"Well, he didn't know he could ask. Of course he would want to see us!"

Mr. Akram shrugged his shoulders. "How was I to know? He never asked."

The chargé d'affaires asked me more questions about my prison experience. Did I have access to a doctor? Was I getting enough to eat? Could I sleep okay?

I answered all his questions as best I could, and then after a while, the Iranian officials started stuffing papers back into their bags and looking at one another. I knew the meeting was nearly over.

The Swiss officials got the message, too.

"Before we leave, I have a few things for you. Your parents asked us to bring you a Bible. It wasn't easy to find an English one, but we managed," David Steiner said, handing me a Gideon Bible, the same Bible found in thousands of hotel rooms all over the United States.

"Thank you," I said. "I really appreciate your looking for this."

Walter Graff stood, picked up a large paper bag from under the table, and handed it to me. "Here are a few items you might need, and some money as well," he said.

As I took the bag, David Steiner looked me in the eye. "Dan," he said, using my first name for the first time, "we are working hard on your case. We are in contact with elements in the Iranian government, both inside and outside Iran, every single day. My staff is dedicated to getting you out of here. Don't give up. We'll be meeting with you again soon."

With that, everyone in the room stood. I shook hands with my two new Swiss friends. The meeting was a ray of hope after all I had been through, and I was overwhelmed at the emotions of relief I was feeling right then. Had they been Americans I would probably have hugged them, but I knew from my father's family that the Swiss are much more reserved, and I didn't want to offend or embarrass either man.

"Okay, Mr. Baumann, come with me," Mr. Akram said in an even voice that I could not read.

I was a bit concerned at what would happen to me now. I had deliberately talked about everything Mr. Akram had told me not to mention. What would be the consequences for such blatant disobedience?

I took one last look at the two Swiss men as I walked out the door.

When we were back on the path to the main prison building, Mr. Akram turned to me. "You didn't follow my instructions," he said flatly.

I didn't know how to answer him. I certainly didn't want to say something that would inflame the situation. After a few steps I said, "I had to answer their questions truthfully. I had no choice."

My interrogator looked at me. "It doesn't matter," he said in an offhanded way. "What's done is done."

I could see in his dark eyes that he meant it. His craggy face seemed to hold no malice toward me. I laughed out loud with relief. It was all a big game to him, and he was being gracious at having lost a round. I wondered what would have happened to me if I'd given in to his intimidation and threats and remained silent, or worse, lied in the meeting? Would he be showing me the same begrudging respect if I'd done what he wanted?

As we walked along, Mr. Akram began chatting with me. He pointed to the main prison building. "Do you know who funded and helped build all this?" he asked.

"No," I replied.

"The Israelis. And do you know who helped them?"

"No," I replied again.

"The government of the United States of America!" he said triumphantly. "It's pretty nice, huh?"

It was a bizarre conversation, almost as if we were two friends strolling around a resort and not an interrogator leading a prisoner back to his cell.

We walked on a little farther, and then Mr. Akram stopped for a moment and looked at me. "Is there anything I can do for you?" he asked without any hint of mockery in his voice.

I felt confident that his offer was sincere, so I said, "Yeah, you can get me into another cell. I hate being so close to the guards. They talk all night."

"Okay, I'll arrange that," he said matter-of-factly.

We began walking again, and soon we arrived back at the entrance to the main building. Instinctively, I pulled my blindfold back on and was led through the corridors to my cell.

Mr. Akram escorted me right inside my cell, where he poked through the bag of items I had been given by the Swiss authorities. He pulled out a razor. "You won't be allowed to have this," he said apologetically. "Good afternoon, Mr. Baumann."

I stood for a long time staring at the bag of goodies on the floor before sitting down cross-legged to examine its contents. From habit, I deliberately went slow as I laid everything out in front of me. I wanted to make the moment last. Three bars of Frigor Swiss chocolate, a can of shaving cream, three *National Geographic* magazines, a bag containing ten bright red apples, and the Gideon Bible. It was all a little overwhelming. My mind could scarcely take in all the new choices I now had. I could eat a whole chocolate bar in one sitting, or I could eat it one square at a time, stretching it out over several days. And I could do the same with the apples. And not only did I have a choice to make about how fast or how slow to eat the chocolate and apples, I also had to make some decisions about what to do with the wrappers. I was already leaning toward rolling the foil paper into small marbles so the Beasleys and Fat Fours could have some more bowling tournaments, not to mention games of tiddlywinks with the apple seeds. I decided a square of chocolate was in order as a celebration.

Later that evening, a guard appeared at my cell door. "Gather your things," he said. "You're moving."

I hurriedly threw my new possessions into the paper bag and pulled on my blindfold. With the bag tucked firmly under my arm, I was led down one corridor and then turned left into another. I heard a cell door creak open, and then I was told I could take off my blindfold.

In less than five minutes I had moved "house" with everything I owned. My new cell was the same basic layout as my previous one. The carpet, though, was more threadbare and stained. I optimistically tried flushing the toilet. It worked no better than the one I had just left.

I pulled my belongings from the bag one at a time and arranged them exactly as they had been in the old cell. No sooner had I finished than peals of laughter reverberated through the wall behind the heating radiator and into my cell. I listened carefully as first two, three, then four people erupted into spirited conversation. These were not prisoners talking, though, and I didn't recognize any of the voices as those of guards. I finally came to the conclusion my cell was located next door to some kind of social room for the mullahs, whose official job was to make better Muslims out of those unfortunate enough to be imprisoned in Evin.

I waited for the noise to die down, but the voices in the next room kept coming and going throughout the night. By the time the breakfast cart arrived at 7 A.M., I was regretting having asked Mr. Akram for a new cell. I couldn't help but wonder if he had deliberately given me a noisier cell. I decided to find out how sincere he had been when he said he wanted to help me. After breakfast I asked the guard to relay the message to Mr. Akram that I wanted to be transferred to another cell away from the noise of gossiping guards and socializing mullahs.

The guard must have relayed my message, because that evening I was moved once again, farther along the same corridor. I could still hear the guards, but the sound of the socializing mullahs had disappeared. I was grateful for the move, but I decided not to push my luck any further. As far as I was concerned, this new cell would do as my new home.

Over the next few days, I repeatedly thanked God for the opportunity to meet with the Swiss authorities. Every time I thought about it, I welled up with emotion and appreciation. Although it had lasted no more than half an hour, it had a profound effect on me. For the first time since being arrested, I knew for certain that I hadn't been forgotten. That realization bolstered my spirit considerably. People on the outside cared about me and were working hard on my behalf. I also now knew I had some rights. I was entitled to a phone call every ten days and the right to get some fresh air each week. And more than that, I had hope that I would soon know what I was being formally charged with and that my case would progress forward to a point where I could prove my innocence.

Three days later, in my sixth week of incarceration, two official-looking documents were delivered to my cell. One document bore the official seal of the Swiss ambassador, and the other had the logo of the American Interest Section of Iran on it. On the first document was a note that read, "Mr. Baumann, please find enclosed two pages. On them write your name, citizenship, the reason you came to Iran, and a brief statement to the effect you are not a spy. Sign the documents and return them to the guard. Kind regards, Mr. Johan Meier, Ambassador."

The guard stood over me as I wrote, urging me to hurry. Within two minutes I scribbled down the requested information, and the guard left with the documents.

As my sixth week in captivity drew to a close, I sat on the floor reading one of the novels given to me by the Iranian guards. They had given me ten books in all. I began by reading *Roots*, but I gave up because of the despair I found in its pages. I then read *Bone Crack* by Dick Francis, a story of a horse trainer. Now I was reading a third book titled *A Coffin from Hong Kong*. While reading helped to pass the time, it could also be disheartening. I would get so caught up in the story I was reading that I would forget I was sitting in a prison cell in Iran. Unfortunately, every time I put the book down, the depressing reality of my grim surroundings came rushing back.

As I sat reading, the room suddenly plunged into darkness. Instead of alerting the guard, I decided to enjoy the darkness and wait for him to peer into my cell on his next round and discover I had no light.

When the guard did come and discover my cell was dark, he grew very agitated. "It has to be fixed from upstairs," he yelled at me through the peephole.

About ten minutes later, I heard a grating noise above my head, and I understood what he had meant. Apparently, the light could be accessed from some kind of crawl space above the ceiling, eliminating the need to enter the cell to fix it. I marveled at the ingenuity of the Israelis and Americans who had planned and built the jail. I just wished it wasn't being used to house one of their citizens.

The light bulb was replaced, and I was getting back to reading when once again I heard a small pop. The room plunged back into darkness. I waited for about an hour this time before the guard discovered I was without light again. I heard feet rustling outside the door to my cell, and then suddenly two guards burst in, their faces red with anger.

"We know what you are doing!" yelled the guard with a chipped front tooth.

"I didn't do anything," I retorted. Inside I was panicking, for these two men were very agitated.

"Don't tell us lies!" screamed the second guard. "We know you're throwing water on the light to put it out."

"I did not," I said, hiding my shaking hands behind my back. "Why would I want to do a dumb thing like that?"

"Of course you did," yelled the chipped-tooth guard. "I know what goes on in this cell. Now stand up and put your hands against the wall."

I did as I was told, trying to look calm and innocent on the outside. On the inside, though, I was shaken, wondering what these angry men might do next. I had been in jail long enough to know that if they said I threw water on my light, then that would become the "truth" of the situation no matter how much I protested my innocence.

After more yelling and poking in an attempt to get me to "confess," the guards left, and once again the light was pulled up through the ceiling and the bulb replaced. When the light was finally lowered back into place, I prayed fervently that the bulb would not blow again. Thankfully it didn't.

SIXTEEN

An Unexpected Conversation

A S I tried to sleep at night, the voices of the guards continued to float into my cell at all hours. At about 9 P.M. on February 20, three or four guards began a lively conversation. I couldn't hear everything they said, but I heard enough to know they were talking about the phone call I was entitled to make. Each guard seemed to be making a case for why one of the others should be the person to take me to the telephone and supervise my call. It seemed everyone had a reason why it should not be him. As I listened, it became clear that someone had authorized my phone call, but the guards were too scared to carry out the order in case I said something I wasn't meant to discuss over the phone.

The conversation went on for an hour or so, sometimes quietly, other times with yelling and heated tempers. Through it all I waited anxiously for someone to step up to the task, but no one did. Finally, the guards' duty shift ended, and with it went my hopes of being allowed to make the legally required phone call.

The next day, though, something positive did happen. I was sitting on the floor holding a "letter" competition between the Beasleys and the Fat Fours. All that was needed to play this game was a line of text. I used one of the *National Geographic* magazines. The two teams would guess which letter, apart from "e," was the most common on a given line. I would then count the two letters the Beasleys and Fat Fours had chosen to see which one was the most common. The team who guessed the letter that occurred the most on that line won the point. It took three points to win a round and seven rounds to win a tournament.

The Fat Fours had just won their third point when the door swung open. "Time for your hour outside," a guard said. "Let's go."

After the telephone call fiasco, getting some fresh air was the last thing I had expected. Hurriedly, I scrambled to my feet, put on my blindfold, and left my cell. I was escorted down the corridor, up a flight of stairs, and along another corridor before coming to a halt in front of a wooden door. I pulled my blindfold off as the guard opened the door, and to my dismay he had led me back to the mop closet.

"Get in," the guard instructed.

I obediently stepped inside.

"You have one hour. I'll be waiting outside," he snarled as he shut and locked the door.

Anger rose within me. I had really gotten my hopes up at having an hour outside with a chance to stretch my legs and walk more than four steps in any direction. Only being allowed to stay longer in the mop closet was not what I had envisioned. However, as I stood staring up at the clouds as they sailed across my tiny patch of sky, I calmed down. The more I studied the sky, the more amazed I was by its vastness and by the greatness of its Creator. Before I knew it, the hour was up, and the guard unlocked the door and gestured for me to come out.

When I returned to my cell, I sat for a long time thinking about the beauty of the sky. After sitting quietly for a couple of hours, I could hear two guards who had started a discussion down the corridor. I strained to hear what they were saying.

"I saw it this morning. The foreigner really did rip the holy book!" one of the guards exclaimed.

I clenched my teeth. It was the same discussion I'd heard before. For some reason the guards were fixated by the idea that I had ripped apart a Bible in my possession, even though it was handed to me that way by the Iranian authorities. I supposed they had ripped it apart sometime between taking it off Glenn and returning it to me. I wanted to put my mouth by the bottom of the door and yell, "It was ripped when you gave it to me, you fools," but I knew it would only inflame the situation and probably get me a severe beating.

"He'll get four more months for that," the guard continued. "His lack of respect for that which is holy is of grave concern."

The other guard laughed. "Of course not!" he exclaimed. "He's got one month to go. That's how long they always keep foreigners."

"Not foreigners who defile holy books," the other guard replied.

As I listened to the one guard's reasoning, I tried to stay calm, but his words about disrespect rang in my ears. He sounded so sure of himself. I had already offended a mullah by a simple mistake. If I were ever convicted of something, I would have another four months tacked onto my sentence for something I didn't do. Why I was actually worried about this, I didn't know. I was already in jail for something I hadn't done!

I paced the floor of my cell, back and forth, four steps at a time. As I did so, I sensed God speak to my heart. "Listen to the second man," He said. "He is the one speaking the truth."

I quickly turned my attention back to the conversation, listening to hear what the second guard, whom I called my "Angel" of hope, had to say. "It's the pattern they always follow," he said. "You wait and see. The American will be gone in a month."

I tried to remember every word the second guard said. Long after they had stopped talking and into the night, I repeated his comments in my mind, praying that I had heard God correctly and that the second guard's prediction that I would be freed within a month was really true.

The following night, four guards congregated in the same spot and began to talk about me again. As I listened, the conversation seemed calm and orderly. I did not hear any of the usual jeering when my name was mentioned.

"Why do you think he came to Iran?" one guard asked. "It's such a dangerous place for an American to be."

I had heard this question discussed many times before. In Iranian culture a topic is discussed until every possible nuance of meaning is explored. But tonight, I listened with unusual interest. Deep down, I felt something different was about to happen.

As I listened, my "Angel" from the night before began to speak. "He's a Christian, and I know what Christians believe."

"You do?" asked one of the other guards, surprised.

"Yes," said my angel. "During the overthrow of the Shah, I knew some Christians who were imprisoned here in Evin. They told me all about their religion."

"Well?" asked another voice.

"Well, they believe that Jesus Christ was the only Son of God, and that He came to earth to show mankind how much God loves them."

I could hardly believe my ears. Listening to them discuss Christianity and the claims of Jesus Christ in the depths of the most notorious high-security prison in all of Iran was a miracle. I listened avidly as Angel went on to describe Jesus' birth, the message of repentance He had preached, and even His death on a cross to save all mankind from their sins. Whenever he paused, one of the other guards would ask a sensible question.

When Angel had finished a very accurate summary of the New Testament message, one of the other guards said, "You mean Christians think God is a God of love?"

"Yes," Angel said, "they do."

"Well," replied the other guard, "how can that be? We don't know anything about God being a God of love. We only know a God of force and control. That's what we've experienced in Islam."

The others murmured in agreement. And then one of them said, "As far as I see it, there is a problem. How can you believe God is one when Jesus is the Son of God and He is also God? That makes two Gods, not one."

I listened carefully to see how Angel, a Muslim himself, would answer this objection, since it is one of the key issues Muslims stumble over when trying to understand Christianity.

There was silence for a moment, and then Angel started out in a confident voice. "These Christians truly believe that God is a God of love, but how can you be a God of love if you are just one? Love is a relationship, and it must exist between persons. They believe that before the beginning of time there was God, but can you be love and express love if you have no one to love? So God is in three parts so that He could demonstrate love."

The longer I sat and listened to this conversation, the more amazed I became. I remembered hearing from a friend that many Anglican bishops had been imprisoned in Evin during the revolution of 1978–79. It was remarkable that I was here listening to a man who remembered in great detail what those Christians had told him about their faith nearly twenty years before. God's plan and purpose were slowly beginning to dawn on me, and I was amazed at how He had orchestrated it all.

I couldn't help but think of Paul's words in 1 Corinthians 3:6: "I planted the seed, Apollos watered it, but God made it grow." I knew being locked up in Evin and being up front about my beliefs had had an impact on the prison. But it was an impact built upon the witness of all the Christians who had gone before me in this place. I began to pray fervently that God would bring some of these guards to know Him as a result of our joint witness.

In-depth conversations among the guards about Christianity went on for the next two weeks, and I listened in to them all. Angel always took the lead, telling the others about what the Christians believed, while the other guards asked him questions.

One night I listened as Angel said, "This foreigner has affected me deeply. He has come here with a purpose and a reason, and he knows he could get killed for it. Would any of us be willing to go to a foreign country to tell others about our God? What would we tell them? This guy has a reason to live and a reason to die. What do we have?"

"Yeah," agreed another guard, "it's strange. I stand by his cell sometimes, and I hear him praying for us! We could have him killed. He's doing all this for love? We know nothing about this God of love, but it sounds very right."

Then Angel said quietly, "I want to become a Christian."

"I do, too," said a second voice. "And I know there is another one who thinks as we do."

"And I don't care what anyone says," Angel went on. "I've heard of a Christian church in town. I'm going to find it." His voice had a determination to it that I hadn't heard before.

"Well, I'm not sure I want to go that far," said the second guard. "Being a Christian in your heart is one thing. Telling everyone else is quite another. You know what could happen if we defy Islam."

"Yes," Angel agreed, "but I don't care who knows or what could happen. I want to find this God of love."

I sat in awe and amazement. "God, is this why you allowed me to be here?" I asked quietly.

Over the next few days, I prayed often for Angel and the other two guards who had made one of the most dangerous of choices, to become a Christian in a Muslim country.

The guards' decisions to become Christians was a bright spot in an otherwise bleak existence. Nothing seemed to be happening with my case. I did not have another visit with the Swiss authorities, and apart from my weekly shower and visit to the mop closet, life had become very monotonous.

On March 2, in my seventh week of incarceration, I was taken to the courthouse again, but even this proved anticlimactic. I sat waiting for five hours before being called into the judge's chamber.

He asked me if I wanted the Iranian government to provide a defense lawyer for my trial. I didn't know what to answer. Of course I would like a *good* defense attorney to handle my case. I would just like to know what I was being charged with first! I knew what their suspicions were, which scared me, but the uncertainty and lack of legal procedure only made me worry all the more. I had great reservations, though, about agreeing to be represented by an Iranian lawyer. He would undoubtedly be working for the government. How could he give me the best defense possible? Would he even want to help me? Perhaps he might even hope that the government proved its case against me. I didn't want to agree to a lawyer who could possibly be detrimental to my case. Neither did I want to agree to a lawyer and give my case some sort of legitimacy. It would only strengthen the false charges they were trying to lay against me. What I really wanted to do was ask the Swiss chargé d'affaires for his advice, but that request was denied.

In the end, after twenty minutes of sitting in the judge's office while he went about his other tasks, I finally decided I had no other choice. Hesitantly, I agreed to have a government-appointed lawyer. A short while later I was climbing back on the bus for the return trip to Evin. The whole trip back I thought about what I had just agreed to, for it could have serious repercussions. I thought I had probably done the right thing, but I wasn't sure.

Later that night, the guards were talking among themselves at the end of the corridor when the head warden arrived on the scene. I knew his voice because I had met him a couple of times. He was older than the other guards, and he always looked scruffy and unkempt, which surprised me in light of his position.

"That American went to court today," the warden said.

"He did?" a guard replied. "What happened?"

"Not much," the warden said, "but they're going to sentence him to eleven months."

I heard Angel chuckle to himself. "No, they're not!" he said. "He'll be out of here within the month. That's how long they keep foreigners."

"Are you saying I'm wrong?" the warden asked with a nasty edge to his voice.

"Well, I don't think he'll be here that long either," another guard said before Angel could answer.

Even though I could not see their faces, I could sense the tension begin to rise.

They argued about my fate for a few minutes, and then the head warden exploded. "No! No!" he yelled. "I'm in charge here, and I'm sick and tired of having a Christian in my prison. He's got to go. I'm taking him somewhere."

"Calm down. He doesn't hurt anyone," Angel said.

The head warden just became more agitated. "I'm never going to let him leave this prison," he said. "He can stay here until he rots. He's not going to the courthouse again. He's not going anywhere. He is a criminal and a Christian, and we are Muslims. Under Islamic law I have the right to kill him myself!"

Terror swept over me. This man was dead serious, and I feared for my life.

I heard Angel trying to calm him down.

Finally, after several more minutes of ranting, the head warden stomped off in the opposite direction, muttering to himself.

I waited tensely through the next day to see if the warden would follow through on his threat. Nothing happened. Later that night, the warden was back talking with the guards about me at the end of the corridor. He was more agitated than he had been the night before. Fortunately the other guards managed to pacify him somewhat, and again he went stomping off. Sleep didn't come easily, and I tossed and turned, wondering what might happen to me the next time the warden came if the other guards couldn't calm him down.

The next night the warden was back at around three o'clock in the morning. I heard him yelling at the top of his voice. "No, no, I am going to kill him right now."

I listened, terrified, as I heard the warden walk into a nearby security office and open a drawer.

Angel screamed at him, "No. No! Put it back. Don't do it! Don't shoot him. Do you know what will happen to you if you do?"

"He's a dead man!" the warden yelled. "I don't care what happens to me. Death to all Christians!"

I spun my head around, looking for a place to hide in my cell. There was none. "God," I prayed frantically, "send your Holy Spirit to calm this situation before it's too late."

I listened to Angel's soothing voice speaking in the corridor outside. "Listen to me. He is a good man."

"Ha," spat the warden. "He is a Christian."

"Yes, he is," Angel agreed, "but he is a man who knows God. I am going to stand in front of his door, and if you want to shoot him, you are going to have to shoot me first."

I stood transfixed, waiting for what would happen next. Would the head warden back down, or would I hear gunshots? The next few seconds seemed to freeze in time and stretch into an eternity.

Thankfully, Angel kept talking, and I prayed for God to intervene and save my life. Somehow Angel managed to reason with the man. After about twenty minutes, I heard the drawer open, and something was dropped into it. I supposed it was the gun. I had escaped death for the night, but I dreaded what might happen the next evening.

Sure enough, the following night the guards were gathered at the end of the corridor talking among themselves when once again the head warden came along. This time, though, one of the guards spoke up first.

"What's really going on?" he asked the warden bluntly.

"What do you mean?" the warden retorted.

"Well," continued the guard, "everything is fine during the day. You don't seem to be worried about the foreigner. But at night you get all worked up about him and want to kill him."

"I don't know what happens, but it's not me," the warden replied.

"What do you mean, 'It's not me'?" Angel asked.

"Well," the head warden said, "every night about ten or eleven a dark force seems to enter me. It takes me over and makes me do things. It gets inside my head. I know it's something to do with demons."

"What makes you say that?" another guard asked.

The head warden let out a long sigh. "I was very young when I first encountered the power of demons. I allowed those forces to enter my life and give me power—not all of the time, but sometimes. When this foreigner came to the prison, I felt a strong demon say to me, 'I want to live inside you because there's someone in this prison I want to destroy.'"

I could hardly believe what I was hearing. I knew many Muslims had a strong belief in Satan and demonic activity. To my horror, the warden was not only a believer in demons but a participator with them as well! "God," I cried out, "protect me from this man who has my life in his hands!"

"Okay, I understand," Angel said matter-of-factly to the warden. "It's not really you, then, who's going crazy late at night."

"No," the warden agreed. "It's this dark force trying to control me more and more."

"Why don't you get rid of it?" Angel asked.

"I'm scared, scared that if I deny access to this spirit, he will turn on me and kill me," the warden said.

After these words, I heard footsteps leading away from my cell, and I knew I was safe for another night. Though I was shaking, I sat there and thanked God for His protection and for how He had used Angel.

The following day passed uneventfully. I spent most of it reading my Bible and meditating and thinking about what might happen that night. The letter to the Philippians, which Paul wrote while he was in prison, came alive to me as I considered my fate. In chapter three, verse eight, Paul wrote, "I consider everything a loss compared to the surpassing greatness of knowing Christ Jesus my Lord, for whose sake I have lost all things. I consider them rubbish, that I may gain Christ."

"Wow," I said to myself, "I am not Paul, but I want to be like him. I want to be able to have the peace and the calmness of God in any situation. I want to count all things, even a warden who wants to kill me, as rubbish for the joy and privilege of knowing Christ."

At about 1 A.M. that night, I needed my new resolve. The warden was back, and he was ranting and raving again about how he wanted to kill me. I was beginning to feel a sense of desperation creep over me when I heard the voice of Angel speaking clearly. "Jesus," he said, "Jesus. In the name of Jesus go." Somewhere he must have heard about the power in the name of Jesus.

Suddenly, I heard the warden give a bloodcurdling scream, and then everything was silent as the warden walked away. Twice more during the night he came back determined to shoot me. Each time I heard Angel saying the name of Jesus, and then the head warden would quiet down.

Over the next two nights, the same incident happened seven or eight times more.

On the fourth night, when the warden came, I heard him say to the other guards, "It's okay. It's over. It's gone." He then went on to say the most amazing things. "I'm sorry," he told the guards. "I don't know what happened to me, but I feel like myself again. I don't hate the foreigner. I never hated the foreigner. In fact, I love this foreigner, and I want to help him."

"Really?" one of the guards asked.

"Yes," the warden said emphatically. "If anyone messes with this foreigner, they will have to answer with me. If he has to stay here a long time, I'm going to take really good care of him."

I sat stunned by what he was saying. God had done much more than my puny faith thought possible!

The warden was true to his word, and prison life became much easier for me to bear. When the guards came by to check on me, they would smile and ask how I was. Some of them would even tell me jokes.

The release in tension was obvious, and it had an immediate effect on my outlook and my health. I started to sleep more soundly at night, and for the first time I actually began to think about my future in prison. I told myself that maybe I would get out of solitary confinement one day and be allowed into a group cell. I could make friends and talk to the other prisoners. Something might be worked out so I could make phone calls home and even receive mail from family and friends. Who knew what possibilities lay ahead? Now that I had experienced God working for good through my imprisonment, it was easier to trust Him with my future.

SEVENTEEN

Freedom

HOT water spilled down on my body. It was March 13, 1997, day sixty-one of my incarceration, and I was enjoying the luxury of an unscheduled shower. Something out of the ordinary was about to happen. As I lathered up, I tried to imagine what it might be. Perhaps I was going to another meeting with officials from the Swiss embassy. Maybe I was going back to court. For a fleeting moment I even entertained the idea that my parents might be waiting for me somewhere in the prison.

"Out now," the guard ordered, not allowing me my usual leisurely shower.

I hopped out, dried off, and put on a clean set of prison pajamas. I then pulled on my blindfold, and the guard led me out of the shower room, along a corridor, and down some stairs to the same holding area where I had waited for the bus to take me to the courthouse twice before.

As I waited, I peered out of the corner of my blindfold. I saw about twenty other prisoners waiting in the area, and none of them had blindfolds on. I slipped mine off, too, and craned my neck above the crowd to look around for Glenn, though I was almost certain he had been released by now.

I noticed my vision was blurry when I looked over toward the wall. I blinked a few times and looked again. It was still blurry. Eight weeks ago I could have easily seen the cracks in that wall. But that was before I'd spent twenty-four hours a day in my tiny cell. From my time working in the hospital in Afghanistan, I knew that eyes needed constant exercise adjusting from objects that are close up to those that are far away. Without something far away to focus on, eyesight can deteriorate. Mine had considerably.

No guards were around, and nothing seemed to be happening. We were all just standing there waiting. As the time passed, I found myself beginning to relax. I smiled and nodded at a few of the other prisoners, and one of them asked me what I was doing in Evin. Other than the prisoner on my first trip to the courthouse, I had not allowed myself to talk to any other prisoners for fear they might be spies. This time, however, the desire to communicate overrode my caution, and I struck up a conversation with the two prisoners nearest me. Much to my surprise, both of them spoke perfect English with an American accent. And once they learned I was American, they were eager to tell me their stories of how they had ended up in Evin Prison.

The taller of the two men told me he had been a surgeon in Irvine, California, while the second man had lived in Westwood, California. I could hardly believe it! Here I was thousands of miles from home, and these two men had lived within fifty miles of my hometown.

I asked the surgeon why he was in prison, but he could not give me a clear answer. He said he had opened his own practice in Tehran, and that he had been accused of harboring Western ideals. Like me, he was hoping his court visits would eventually lead to some concrete charges he could defend himself against.

Unlike the surgeon, the second prisoner knew exactly why he had ended up in jail. He had come back to Iran to start his own business, and having adapted to the Western way of life during his time in the United States, he refused to pay the customary bribes and kickbacks that were part of the Iranian system. His refusal to cooperate had enraged a local official, who fabricated some charge against the man and had him arrested and sent to prison.

We continued to talk, and soon other prisoners joined in the conversation, eager to tell their stories. As I listened to each one, I discovered that most of the prisoners were being detained because of money issues. They hadn't paid the right kickback, or they owed some obscure tax that they'd had no idea was due. A young man about my age confessed he was in prison for watching an American video— nothing X-rated, just a family movie! I was thankful I had gotten rid of the copy of the *Jesus* video before crossing into Iran.

Everyone seemed very interested in my case. A foreigner in Evin was a rarity, though one of the prisoners told me there had been an African-American man in the prison, but he had not been seen for a few months. We stood talking together for nearly half an hour before the prison bus drove up. As we all climbed aboard, I found out that we were heading for the courthouse. I had been told nothing and began to wonder if any new developments had taken place.

When we arrived at the courthouse, we were led into the same holding area I'd been held in on my previous two visits. This time, though, we were allowed to walk around and talk quietly to one another. For some reason, there seemed to be a relaxed atmosphere.

After a while, other people, non-prisoners, were allowed to join us in the holding area. Women sobbed and wailed as they were reunited with their husbands and sons. I couldn't help but overhear some of their conversations.

"How can the children and I go on without you? You must come home! We have nothing in the house to eat," one woman pleaded, holding a skinny two-year-old in her arms. "There is nothing more I can do from in here. You must raise the money. Ask my brother. He can give you more," her husband replied.

I knew this conversation and the others I heard like it were referring to the way Iranian prisoners could buy their freedom. The amount they needed to pay was set at a special hearing. It was outright bribery, and everyone knew it. But it was also how the court system survived. The court wanted the prisoners to pay the bribe and buy their way out of jail, and the longer a prisoner stayed in jail, the more desperate they became, pressuring family members into helping raise the bribe money. It was a vicious cycle that only served to keep the whole system corrupt.

The reunions of the prisoners with their families went on through lunchtime, and it was 2 P.M. before I was called into the small waiting room beside the judge's office. The court interpreter was seated inside, looking as insolent as ever.

I nodded to him, and he smiled back as he pointed to a poster of Khomeini on the wall. "So what do you think of Khomeini, Dan?" he asked.

I knew I would have to answer very carefully. "Well, he was your leader. I honor the leaders of your country."

"No," the interpreter pushed me. "Tell me what you really think. Do you like him? Do you appreciate what he has done for our country?"

I had been in the room with this man for less than a minute, and already I was tired of him.

"Yes," I replied in my most passive voice, "but it doesn't matter what I think. I honor him as your leader." I hoped my answer would close the matter, but the interpreter appeared determined to goad me into saying something I would regret.

"Mr. Baumann, I order you to tell me the truth. What do you think?" he demanded.

I stared at the man.

"You do not have the right to remain silent. You must answer my question!" he snapped.

I decided not to say another word to him. I would rather be beaten for not cooperating than tell this man what I really thought about Khomeini.

Finally, after about half an hour of uneasy silence, a secretary opened the adjoining door to the judge's office and called us in.

"He won't answer my questions," the interpreter blurted out as we entered the room.

The judge gave him a withering look and motioned for me to sit down.

"So how are they treating you in prison?" he asked in Farsi.

"Fine," I replied, "though I am lonely. I would like to be transferred to a cell with other men if that is possible," I told him.

The judge jotted down a note and went on. "Are you able to go out in the fresh air for an hour a week, Mr. Baumann?"

"Yes," I replied, though a part of me wanted to tell him the rest of the story, that outside really meant a roofless mop closet, but I sensed it wasn't the right time to do so.

"And what is your address in America if I wanted to send something there?" he asked.

I had no idea what he might want to send, but I gave him my parents' mailing address in Colorado.

After he had written it down, the judge abruptly stood up. "I am sorry, but I'm very busy today," he said. "Can you come back and see me the day after tomorrow? I have more I want to talk to you about."

"Sure," I replied, glad for another outing to look forward to.

Turning to the interpreter, the judge said, "I will escort Mr. Baumann back to the guards. You may go."

I could tell the interpreter was not happy about being dismissed, but he turned and left. I followed the judge out of the room. The holding area was empty now, and I guessed everyone was being loaded back onto the bus. He motioned me to the right and began speaking as we walked along.

"I am sorry I did not have more time to spend with you," he said in Farsi, and then he switched to English. "And by the way, Mr. Baumann, I am going to help you."

"Really?" I said, not sure what to think. We were nearing the door to the courtyard where the bus was parked. A guard stood waiting for me.

"Yes, Mr. Baumann, I am going to help you. Have a good evening. Good-bye."

That night I lay awake smiling to myself. For the first time in a long time, I felt some real hope. I truly believed the judge was serious. From what I could tell, it appeared he really did want to help me. Did it mean I might get to move into a cell with other prisoners and end my solitary confinement? Maybe he was going to authorize more visits with the embassy officials. Or could it possibly mean he was actually going to help get me released?

The next day, the Muslim Holy Day, passed quietly. The following morning, Saturday, I was taken back to the holding area to await the prison bus for my trip back to see the judge. No other prisoners were around, and the guard allowed me to take off the blindfold. When the bus pulled up, I walked over to it. I was stunned to see a black man climbing aboard ahead of me. He had been led out of a side door. Could this be the American man the Iranian prisoner had told me about on a previous ride to the courthouse?

I climbed aboard the bus and sat down beside the man. "Hey, do you speak English?" I asked.

"Yeah, I speak English," he said with a southern accent.

"Where are you from?"

"Louisiana," he said. "How about you?"

"California," I replied. "My name's Dan Baumann. What are you doing here?"

"The name's Joseph Morris," he said. "My visa got all messed up. I've been in here fifteen months so far."

I felt my jaw drop. Fifteen months! Just as I was trying to process this information, a guard walked up to the bus and ordered Joseph off. Then, as if on cue, a group of prisoners emerged from the building and got on the bus. I watched as Joseph Morris was led away and another man took his seat beside me. I recognized the man from the court-house who had promised me the new socks several weeks before. He was sitting in the seat right behind me.

Once the old Mercedes bus drove off, the man tapped me on the shoulder. "Hello, my friend. These are for you," he said, handing me a black ball. I quickly unfolded it, discovering a brand-new pair of black socks, the kind with heels in them and ribbing around the ankles. It was almost too good to be true.

I kicked off my orange sandals and pulled off my old, holey socks. I slid my feet into the new socks. They were smooth and warm, and I sat for a full minute just concentrating on how wonderful they felt. I thanked the man for his kindness and generosity, telling myself this could well be a good sign for the rest of the day ahead.

As we drove along, my feet snug and warm in the new socks, I thought about Joseph Morris. What had that been about? Had the prison authorities deliberately brought him to the bus so we could talk?

And if so, what was the point? Was it to scare me? Was it to discourage me? If he'd been here fifteen months for a complication with his visa, I probably could get even more time. I didn't know, but I wished I'd had more time to talk to him.

Finally, the bus pulled up to the courthouse for what proved to be a long day of waiting for me. It seemed as though every hour I was transferred from one room to another and told to sit down on this chair or stand up by that wall. By two o'clock, I was feeling very frustrated. It was about then that I spotted the judge. He was walking toward me, flanked by two mullahs, their white turbans bobbing on their heads with each step. Before they got to me, though, they all turned into the next room, where I could hear parts of their conversation through the open door.

"He worked in a hospital in Afghanistan, helping the poor," said a voice I recognized as that of the judge. "He is a good man, and I will help him."

I couldn't catch the rest of the conversation, but I had heard enough to buoy my spirits.

A few minutes later, the judge came out a side door into the room where I was waiting. He smiled. "Mr. Baumann, I am so sorry. I have been very busy today as well. Would you be kind enough to come back tomorrow?"

"Sure," I replied, thinking how he sounded like a friend asking me over for coffee, when in reality I was a prisoner with no say in where I went and when.

On the bus trip back to the prison, I tried not to replay the conversation in my mind. I wanted to look at the countryside out the window while I had the opportunity. There would be plenty of time later to try to figure out what the judge might be up to.

That night, as I went over the day's events, I sifted through two very different experiences. First there was Joseph Morris, the African-American man on the bus. He had been in Evin Prison for fifteen months for a visa violation. Who was I kidding? How much longer would a person get for supposedly being a CIA spy? But then I thought about the judge's optimistic words. If anyone had the power to help me, he surely did. But did he just say those things to give me a false hope? Was he a cat and I the mouse? Was he just toying with me for his own amusement?

I had no answers to these troubling questions, but I couldn't stop my mind from churning on them most of the night. By 2 A.M. I was totally exhausted and turned to prayer. "Okay, God," I said, "I acknowledge that you are the boss. I am your servant. When I gave my life to you, I told you that you could do what you wanted with me. It's not about my life and what I want. It's all about you, Lord. Do your will in my life. If I have to stay here forever, so be it."

I prayed on until I fell asleep around 4 A.M. Two hours later I awoke to the squeaking wheels of the breakfast cart.

I had just finished my breakfast when three guards burst into my cell. "Hurry, hurry," they said. "Get your things."

It took me a moment or two to react. I looked around the cell. I certainly didn't have much to gather up: my underwear, neatly rolled into a ball for a game of bowling, my Bible, books, and a few eating utensils. After putting on my blindfold, one of the guards took hold of my wrist and led me away.

When I took the blindfold off, I was standing in the same room where Glenn and I had been processed into Evin Prison, fifty-nine days before.

Another guard handed me a trash bag tied with a yellow ribbon. "Put these things on," he said.

I pulled open the bag. It was the same bag I had put my belongings into that first night I arrived at Evin. Inside were my shirt, pants, and shoes. Nothing else. My heart beat wildly as I stripped in double-quick time and put on my own clothes. I had fantasized for so long about once again wearing my own clothes, clothes that fit comfortably. As I pulled on my jeans, though, I groaned. Instead of a snug fit, they hung baggy from my hips. Without a belt, I had to keep hitching them up so they didn't fall right off. Even my shoes were loose on me. I hadn't realized how much weight I had lost.

"Here, sign this," the guard said, thrusting in front of me the list I had written when I put my belongings in the bag so many weeks ago.

I signed the paper, despite the fact that most of my belongings were missing. The guard then handed me a stamp pad and told me to put my thumbprint on the paper as well. I did as I was instructed.

Once I was dressed and had signed the paper, I was whisked out of the room and put on the prison bus.

All the way to the courthouse, my mind kept going down two wildly different tracks. On the one track, I told myself I would be a free man by tonight. And on the other track, I told myself they were simply moving me to another prison, or worse, I was on the way to my execution. I had no way of resolving the conflict between these two scenarios as I mulled them over in my mind. Only time would tell, and I waited anxiously to see where the bus would take me.

Fortunately, it took me to the courthouse, where I was taken into the holding area with the other prisoners. At around 9 A.M., we were given a bathroom break. When I returned, I was taken to the judge's office. The judge was not there, but his secretary was, and he treated me like a guest, even providing me with a cup of hot tea to drink.

"Why are you in your clothes today, Mr. Baumann?" he asked as he handed me the tea. He had a gleam in his eye as he spoke.

I tried my hardest not to get too excited, but it was hard not to imagine I was about to be released.

Finally the judge entered the office. He stopped and spoke to his secretary. "Is everything taken care of?" I heard him ask.

"Yes," the secretary replied.

"Good," the judge said, and then he turned to me and said matter-of-factly, "Okay, let's go, Mr. Baumann. Please come with me."

I followed him out of the office, through the holding area where the other prisoners were seated, and up to a set of double frosted-glass doors. A red line was painted in front of the doors, and a guard sat beside it. The judge nodded to the guard and then pushed the doors open. I followed him through, and in an instant I was in another world. I was in a huge reception area with beautiful Persian carpets on the floor and ornately carved panels on the walls. A long, dark polished wood table sat in the center of the room, and five mullahs sat behind it watching me as I entered. The judge kicked off his sandals and motioned for me to do the same with my shoes. We then slowly approached the table. By then my heart had started to race. Something important was about it happen.

One of the mullahs stood to meet us.

"Is everything ready?" the judge asked him.

"Yes, everything is ready. Come."

The mullah led us through another door and into an opulent office. It had a huge sitting area with a row of chairs along one wall. In front of each chair was a small table, and on each table were a gilt-edged china plate and a basket of fruit. The judge sat down in one of the chairs.

At the end of the office was an ornate desk, and behind it sat another mullah. I had just finished acknowledging the mullah with a nod, when a European man about sixty-five, dressed in gray pants and a navy blue jacket with a yellow-and-red tie, walked up to me. Near him was a young Iranian woman with the traditional black scarf wrapped around her head.

"Hello, Mr. Baumann. I'm Mr. Meier, Swiss ambassador to Iran. It is a pleasure to meet you," he said, thrusting out his hand.

"It's a pleasure to meet you, too, sir," I said, shaking his hand heartily.

He pointed to a chair, and I sat down. Soon another woman entered the room with a dictation pad in hand. The judge began to talk to the mullah while I sat quietly and listened. I gathered from the conversation that this mullah was head judge of all the courts of Iran, which made him a very powerful man. They discussed the contents of some sort of formal letter, how it should be worded, and who would translate it into English.

"Could you read it aloud to me, please," the Swiss ambassador asked.

"Certainly," the judge replied. He began reading the document that was written in high Persian.

Unfortunately, I couldn't understand a word of it. I must have looked frustrated, because the young woman who had accompanied the ambassador leaned over to me and said, "I'll interpret it for you."

She picked up a copy of the document and began to read quietly to me. "Because of our commitment to the Swiss government and our friendship with the Swiss government, we choose to forget about Daniel

Baumann's file, and we choose to hand Daniel Baumann over to the authority of the Swiss ambassador. Mr. Baumann will thereby be at the call of the Swiss ambassador until he is able to secure his exit from the country."

My body reacted before my mind had fully comprehended the words that were being read to me. Tears spilled down my cheeks. I was a free man again! I was no longer prisoner number fifty-eight. Never again would I be going back to Evin Prison.

I turned to the judge. He had a broad smile on his face, a look of triumph, for which I was immensely grateful.

I stayed in the office for another hour, though I don't remember much of what transpired during that time. I was too overcome by the news of my pending freedom. However, I did manage to eat an apple and an orange, and I deliberately left the seeds and the apple core on the gilt-edged china plate. The Beasleys and the Fat Fours would not be needing them for any more games.

Finally, the ambassador stood up, and everyone else followed his lead. He shook hands with each person in the room, thanking them for their help in resolving the situation. He then walked over to me. "Mr. Baumann," he said in a determined voice, "you are coming with me."

"Yes, sir," I replied.

We walked to the door and slipped on our footwear. As we were doing so, the head judge of Iran talked to the ambassador in Persian.

The hairs on the back of my neck stood up. Something was wrong.

"No," I heard the ambassador say firmly. "I will take Mr. Baumann with me now."

The mullah shook his head. "You have to take this letter with you, and it will take us half an hour to translate."

"I don't have half an hour," the ambassador answered firmly. He then looked the mullah right in the eyes. "You will have to deliver it to me."

The mullah backed down. "Yes, we will do that," he said.

Mr. Meier turned to me and said, "Mr. Baumann, we need to leave now."

I turned to follow, but just as I did, the judge walked up to me. "Good-bye," he said.

I reached out to shake his hand, but he extended both arms and drew me into a big hug. Then he kissed me, first on my left cheek, then the right, and then the left again. Tears welled in my eyes as I began to comprehend the significance of what he had just done. In Iranian culture only people of equal righteousness give each other three kisses. By his actions, the judge was saying to me, "You are my friend. You do not have sin in your life." I was overwhelmed by his generosity of spirit.

As the judge stepped back, I thought to myself, *God, you said I was to follow the way of love, and through this experience you have changed Iranian lives. You brought three guards to yourself. You changed the heart of a man from wanting to kill me to wanting to help me, and you gave me favor with this judge. Thank you.*

The ambassador grabbed me by the hand, and together we walked out of the office. The young woman interpreter followed us. We stood waiting for an elevator in the hallway, and as we did, a guard eyed me suspiciously. And no wonder! I caught a glimpse of my reflection in the stainless-steel doors of the elevator. My hair was matted, and my clothes were crumpled and baggy on me. I was a sight!

Finally, the elevator arrived, and we stepped in. When the doors opened one floor below, I quickly followed the Swiss ambassador past more guards and out into the parking lot. He walked briskly to a dark gray Toyota Landcruiser and nodded at the driver. Mr. Meier and I climbed into the backseat while the interpreter got into the front beside the driver.

"Let's get out of here," the ambassador said with urgency in his voice.

I quickly locked my door as we drove off. I was free at last.

EIGHTEEN

Out of Iran

RELIEF surged through me as the Landcruiser wove its way through the busy traffic. As I looked at the red-and-white flags fluttering on both front fenders, I was overwhelmed by my sudden and unexpected change of circumstances.

"It should take about thirty minutes to get back to my residence," Mr. Meier said, peering impatiently out the window.

As we rode along, I thought of Glenn. "Glenn Murray, the South African guy I was imprisoned with. Did he get out?" I asked.

"Yes," the ambassador replied. "He was released on February 18, over a month ago now. I believe he is back in South Africa putting pressure on his government to intervene on your behalf with the Iranian government."

I was glad to learn Glenn was safe. Now we were both free.

As I thought about Glenn, another thought occurred to me. "What day is it?" I asked.

"Sunday, March 16," the ambassador replied.

"And what time is it?"

"It's eleven o'clock," Mr. Meier said, checking his watch.

It had been eleven o'clock when I walked into the Office of Aliens, sixty-three days before. As I thought about it, I felt goose bumps rise all over my body. It was exactly nine weeks, not only to the day, but also to the hour since I had been detained. What was amazing and what overwhelmed me was that God had told me at the beginning I would be in prison for nine weeks. Uncontrollable sobs welled up within me.

As I cried, I knew the ambassador would assume I was overcome at finally receiving my freedom, but that wasn't it at all. I was overcome with the faithfulness of God. He said He would carry me through, and He had. During the darkest times He had always been there. Even during my attempted suicide and those terrifying nights when the head warden almost killed me, God had protected me. I knew many people had been working for my release, including the man sitting beside me, but there was no escaping the perfect timing of it all. God had done exactly what He promised He would do, even though I had doubted Him many times.

Finally, the Toyota glided through the wrought-iron gates of the ambassador's residence. As the gates closed behind me, for the first time in weeks I felt completely safe. When the vehicle came to a halt, Mr. Meier ran inside the residence to get a camera. He emerged moments later followed by a maid and ready to shoot off a roll of film to document my freedom. The two of us posed together in the carefully manicured garden.

When the roll of film had been shot off, I followed the ambassador into the residence. A butler opened the door for us, and Mr. Meier stopped and introduced me. "This is Mr. Baumann," he said. "He is my honored guest. Get him anything he asks for."

The butler nodded and announced lunch would be served in an hour.

I followed the ambassador into a huge foyer.

"I will show you to your room," he said as I stood taking in the grandeur of the place.

A grand piano sat in the corner, and expensive furniture filled every room. The floors were of polished wood and marble, with hand-woven

Persian rugs scattered around on them. On a small table off to the right I spotted a cordless telephone. "Can I call my family?" I asked eagerly.

"Sure, why not?" Mr. Meier replied. "But don't say too much. Every phone call out of here is carefully monitored by the Iranian authorities."

"I'll be brief," I assured him, calculating that it would be about midnight back home in Colorado.

My hands trembled as I dialed the number. As I heard the phone ring on the other end, I told myself I would be quick and as unemotional as possible.

"Hello, Gunila Baumann," I heard the heavily accented voice of my mother say.

"Hi, Mom," I said. "It's me, Daniel."

"Hello, son," she replied cautiously, and I realized she didn't know where I was calling from.

"It's okay, Mom," I said. "I'm out of prison. I'm at the Swiss ambassador's residence."

I heard my mother call to my father. "Hans! It's Dan. He's been set free! Praise God!" she yelled over the phone.

I laughed out loud. That was my mother. "I've been released. I'm fine. I'll be flying to Europe in the next few days. I'll call you back later with the details. I just wanted you to know that I am safe. I have to go now. I love you both," I said, aware that my voice was choked with emotion.

"We love you, son," my mother replied.

As soon as I hung up from talking with my mother, the maid took me to the room I would be staying in until my departure. When she closed the door as she left, I couldn't stop staring at the bed. It was so high and had a fluffy comforter and four feather pillows. It was a stark contrast to the threadbare carpet and old blankets I had been sleeping on for the last few months. I lay down on the bed just to see how soft it felt, even though I was too exhilarated to try to sleep.

Soon the lunch bell rang, and I washed my face and hurried downstairs. Waiting for me at the bottom of the stairs was David Steiner, chargé d'affaires with the Swiss embassy, who had come to visit me in prison. I greeted him warmly, and we sat down together at the lunch table.

The table looked as though it were set for a dinner party. Beside each place setting was a row of spoons, forks, and knives, along with several glasses.

The maid brought out a bowl of steaming hot French onion soup and placed it in front of me.

"Help yourself, Mr. Baumann," the ambassador said.

For a moment I couldn't think straight. I couldn't remember which spoon to use. I decided I should ask rather than make a fool of myself. I leaned over to the ambassador and said, "Excuse me, but which spoon should I use for the soup?"

The ambassador chuckled. "Mr. Baumann," he said, "you are a free man. Use whatever spoon you like."

I chose the one closest to me and proceeded to eat the most delicious soup I had ever tasted. As we ate, the ambassador and David Steiner peppered me with questions about my prison experience. They wanted to know everything I had experienced.

"When you were interrogated, how did you decide what to say and what not to say?" the ambassador asked as the maid continued to bring more food.

I looked him squarely in the eye. "You know, Mr. Ambassador, from the very beginning I purposed to be honest. I chose to tell them the whole truth, even if they killed me for it."

"Ah, that was such a good move, Mr. Baumann," he said. "It made it much easier for us to help you, since we were able to corroborate what you were telling your interrogators. Who told you to do that?"

"Jesus Christ," I replied.

"Jesus Christ?" echoed the ambassador.

"Sure," I said. "He was with me the whole time."

I told both men the story of how God had been faithful to me, even though I had doubted Him often. They listened attentively.

When lunch was over, Mr. Meier suggested I go upstairs to my room for an hour or so, after which he promised to take me to the embassy, where I could meet all the people who had worked so hard to secure my release.

I wandered upstairs and went into the bathroom. When I stepped on the scale, it registered 151 pounds. During my time in Evin, I had lost 40 pounds. For a few moments, I stood looking at myself in the mirror. I was badly in need of a shave and a haircut, but I decided to stay just the way I was until after I had met the people at the embassy who had worked countless days to make this moment become a reality.

I walked back into the bedroom, but I couldn't stay there. Those prolonged days of solitary confinement had taken a toll on me, and I desperately needed to be with people. I went back downstairs and struck up a conversation with the maid.

An hour later, we were off to the embassy. Even though I was riding in an official embassy vehicle, I still felt uneasy about leaving the security of the Swiss ambassador's residence. However, my unease was soon laid to rest when I finally met the people who had worked so hard on my behalf. Everyone was so kind and understanding as they gathered around and asked me questions. I told them all the highs and lows of my experience in Evin Prison. By the time I had finished, we were all crying.

"You had a death sentence on your head," summed up one woman. "You were supposed to die, but we all beat the system."

Inside, I knew that God had used them to "beat the system," but for His higher purposes. His Word had been made real to those guards, showing them that He truly was a God of love and One who could radically change lives.

Everyone could sense the triumph in the room.

As I mingled and talked with different people, I learned more of the particular facts about my case. I was amazed to what lengths these people had gone to secure my freedom. I was overwhelmed with gratitude to God and to them for the commitment they had all made. Among the many other things the ambassador had done, he had taken time out of his busy schedule to fly to Afghanistan, where he searched for records of my work at the hospital.

I was also given an inch-thick stack of photocopied letters that people had written to me. The originals had been forwarded on to Evin for me, but I had not received any of them. I flicked through the stack, recognizing many of the names there. I read one of the letters from my sister Tina. In it she told me she'd given birth to a baby boy in February. She and her husband had named him Caleb Daniel after me. For about the hundredth time that day, my eyes welled up with tears.

There were also many letters from people I did not know, people who had heard through their church or prayer group that I was in prison and had written to encourage me. The genuine concern of such Christian strangers from all over touched me deeply. Even in my darkest hours, I had not been alone. I had been bathed in prayer from all over the world.

I spent the next two days at the ambassador's residence while he made plans for me to leave Iran. During most of this time, my emotions were raw. If I heard a sound, the screeching of tires outside, for example, I jumped, wondering if the police were coming to take me back to Evin. I also worried that the trees in the garden were bugged and that the butler was an Iranian spy. I hardly slept at night, and strangely, in the early hours of the morning, I would miss my prison cell. Part of me longed to be back in that confined space where everything was orderly and I had no responsibilities. Now that I was free, even the smallest decisions were agony to make. My comfort zone had been reduced so drastically during my imprisonment that my newfound freedom brought its own set of psychological and emotional adjustments.

The day after I arrived at the residence, I was told I had to go to an Iranian government office to secure my exit visa. After much protest and prayer, I finally agreed to go, but I was a nervous wreck. The ambassador assured me it was nothing more than a technical detail and that the office I was going to had nothing to do with the prison or the justice department. One of the embassy officials drove me to the office, and as we got closer, I could see it was only a short distance away from the building where all my problems had begun. No matter how much they had assured me that everything would go fine, my heart began to race. For some reason, foreign embassy officials were not allowed into the building where the office was located, so I had to go in on my own.

The embassy car pulled to a halt outside the front door of the building, and with knots in my stomach, I climbed out and went inside. On the second floor, I found the office I was looking for, and to my relief everything was in order. An official was waiting there for me with the papers in hand that needed my signature to obtain the exit visa. I signed the papers and gingerly handed over my passport. I waited nervously, and a couple of minutes later, the official handed my passport back with an exit visa stamped in it.

With my passport in hand, I ran down the stairs as fast as I could, not wanting to give anyone the opportunity to grab me and whisk me back to jail. I burst through the front door of the building and almost dived into the embassy vehicle, a broad grin on my face. I had made it. I had my exit visa, my passport, and I was still free!

After dinner on the second night, the ambassador seemed to be a little agitated. I heard him making a number of phone calls in his office. When he emerged, he looked shaken.

"Dan," he said, "I have to be honest with you. Your release from prison was signed by one of the highest-ranking members of the Iranian government, but many of the people under him are not happy about his decision." His voice grew more serious as he went on. "By law we cannot escort you out to the door of the airplane. We can get you safely to the immigration checkpoint, but after that, you will be on your own."

"Is that going to be a problem?" I asked, my mouth suddenly dry.

"Not necessarily," the ambassador went on, "though there is a portion of the government that is upset that you are free. They would love to get you back in their grasp and make a political scapegoat out of you. I am trying to make sure that all the police and security guards from the immigration checkpoint to the airplane know about you and are willing to let you pass."

This new turn of events upset me greatly. I wanted to stay in the Swiss embassy forever. As long as I remained within its walls, I was safe. The Iranian government had to honor the diplomatic immunity of the embassy grounds. "So it's not over?" I finally said.

"No," the ambassador replied. "It won't be over until you set foot on European soil. But don't worry. You will be doing that very soon. I have decided that since everything is in place, we should move now. Waiting longer may complicate your departure. You will be flying out later tonight on Lufthansa. We can't afford to wait until Thursday for the Swiss Air flight. The political tide can change suddenly here."

The ambassador went over the plan with me. Thanks to him, my passport now had all the correct visas and stamps in it. An hour later, I was headed for the airport with a consular official from the embassy and his driver. The consular official assured me I should have no trouble at the immigration checkpoint. After I was through the checkpoint, I was to wait in the transit area until my flight was called and then walk directly out onto the tarmac and board the plane.

"Nothing should go wrong," he assured me. "We will all wait here in the car for a few minutes so the timing is right. Once you get on the plane, we want it to take off as soon as possible."

I tried to stay calm, but my stomach was in a knot, and I felt like throwing up. I was about to run the gauntlet, and no one could completely assure me of the outcome.

After a few minutes, the driver parked the embassy vehicle, and the consular official got out and looked around. He gestured for me to follow him. Gingerly, I climbed out, leaving the security of the Swiss flag behind me.

We walked into the terminal building, and he pointed to the line where I needed to stand. "I will stand here until I see you get on the plane," the consular official said, gently pushing me forward. "Good luck. Call the ambassador as soon as you land in Frankfurt."

I reached out and shook the man's hand, wondering what to say. "Thank you" seemed too inadequate for all the work the Swiss embassy had done on my behalf to secure my freedom. But I couldn't think of anything better, so I said it anyway.

I took my place in line, trying desperately not to think of the last immigration line I had stood in. Within a couple of minutes, I was at the head of the line. An immigration officer checked my paper work, grunted, and then waved me on.

I was now all on my own. I waited for about half an hour in the transit area before the flight was called and we could board the plane. I tried not to look too nervous as I waited. It wasn't all that easy to do, though, given the number of soldiers with automatic weapons patrolling the area. When the flight was finally called, I headed for the security check. After being body searched, I followed the other passengers out the door.

I hesitated as I walked toward the tarmac. Now would be a perfect moment to ambush me, I thought. To my great relief, nothing happened, and I climbed the stairs to the Airbus A320. As I crossed the threshold of the door to the aircraft, I knew I was on German property.

I squeezed into a window seat next to a very large man. I was one of the last passengers to board the plane, and I watched with relief as the cabin door was closed and take-off procedures began immediately. As the jet engines started to spin, so did my imagination. I couldn't help it. I fretted that the man beside me might be a government agent sent to bring me back. Perhaps other spies had been planted on the plane and had orders to stalk me across Europe. I tried to laugh at my paranoid thoughts, but given the horrendous ordeal I had been through for the last nine weeks, those thoughts had a powerful hold over me.

I watched as we taxied past the terminal building. I could not see the consular official, but I was grateful he was there watching the plane take off.

Once we reached the end of the runway, I heard the jet engines begin to scream, and the Airbus raced forward. Moments later we were in the air. We were still in Iranian airspace, though, and I anxiously watched the screen in the front of the plane. A thin gray line marked our projected path, while a green line indicted how far we had traveled.

As I watched the green line mark off the miles we had covered, I thought to myself, *I'm not free yet. All it would take is a medical emergency, and I would be right back on Iranian soil.*

No sooner had I thought it than the airplane's speaker crackled to life with an urgent-sounding voice. "If there are any medical personnel on board, could you please come to the back of the plane immediately."

My whole body was shaking as I turned to try to find out what was going on. As I craned to see, several people got out of their seats and made their way toward the back of the plane. Panic suddenly gripped me. I had to think of something. I was not going back to Iran for a medical emergency or any other reason.

I unfastened my seatbelt and squeezed out into the aisle. I had to find out what was going on and, if needed, to pray for whoever was sick.

When I got to the back of the plane, I saw a woman lying on the floor. A stewardess and two passengers were bent over her. A second stewardess intercepted me. "Are you a doctor?" she asked.

"No. I just need to know what's going on. Are we turning back?" I said, hearing the irrationality in my voice.

"Please return to your seat, sir," she said coolly. "We can take care of everything."

I stood staring for a long moment before I walked back down the aisle.

I took my seat again and fixed my eyes on the green line on the screen in front. I expected to see it curve around as the plane headed back to Tehran. Instead, it kept going straight ahead, following our projected flight path to Frankfurt, Germany. The medical emergency seemed to continue on in the back of the plane, but I breathed a sigh of relief when the green line indicated we had crossed the border into Turkish airspace. We were now closer to Ankara than Tehran if we had to make an emergency landing.

Finally, the medical emergency seemed to pass. The woman got off the floor and back into a seat, and the rest of the flight continued on uneventfully all the way to Frankfurt. When we finally touched down in Frankfurt, those passengers who were in transit were invited to a buffet breakfast in the transit lounge while the plane was refueled.

I walked off the plane, glad to stretch my legs. Suddenly, I spotted a German policeman with a gun. Before I could stop myself, I dashed for cover behind a pole. I peered out to see if the policeman was watching me. When I realized what I had done, it took all my mental strength to make myself step out and walk past the officer to the transit lounge. On the way, I spotted a telephone and remembered my promise to call the Swiss ambassador as soon as I arrived. I dialed the number of his residence and spoke to his maid, since he was not at home. We had a brief conversation, and she was glad to hear everything had gone as planned.

I was one of the last passengers to arrive in the transit lounge. By then most of the others had gone through the buffet line and divided into two groups. A group of Iranians sat at one table and the Europeans at the other. As I loaded my plate up with bacon and scrambled eggs and poured a glass of orange juice, I decided I would sit with the Iranians. After I introduced myself, they began asking me questions in Farsi.

"How long were you in Iran?" one man asked.

"About three months," I replied, watching some eyebrows rise.

"That's a long time. Where did you stay?" another man asked.

I thought for a moment, "Oh, I toured around for a couple of weeks, and then I went to Evin."

The first man gave a nervous cough. "Evin?" he repeated. "You don't mean Evin Prison, do you?"

"Yes, that's where I stayed," I said, taking a sip of orange juice.

I was immediately deluged with questions: Why was I in Evin? How was I treated there? Why hadn't they read about my case in the newspapers? What was I going to do now?

I answered their questions as best I could, and when I was finished, they all sat in silence for a moment.

Finally one of the men spoke. "On behalf of our country," he said, shaking his head in dismay, "I would like to offer you our extreme apologies. I hope that you do not equate the way the government has treated you with the hearts of the Iranian people."

I looked the man in the eye. "No, I do not," I replied from the bottom of my heart. "I know the Iranian people are warm, hospitable, and wonderful, and I hope to go back to your country one day"

NINETEEN

Home at Last

I T was midmorning when I finally stepped off the plane in Zurich. My aunt Lotti was there waiting for me, along with an official from the Swiss government. After some preliminary questions, I was allowed to leave with my aunt.

The next two weeks were a blur of events and images. I walked in the Swiss Alps, marveling at the wide-open spaces and awesome stillness I found there. Strangely, I found myself turning down home-cooked meals in favor of McDonald's. I was amazed at the freedom I had to walk in and out of shops as I pleased. I also talked to my sisters on the phone and went back to the airport to meet my mother and father, who had flown in from the United States. I received phone calls, faxes, and e-mails from around the world. My mother told me it had been estimated that over one million people had prayed for my release. I was humbled and amazed by the outpouring of love and concern from Christians all around the world, and I wished I could thank each one in person.

During my time in Switzerland, I traveled to France, where I checked myself into La Ruche, a small center that specializes in debriefing people who have been in crisis situations. My sister Lis convinced me that I fit this category, and as soon as I arrived, I was glad I had come. Professional counselors helped me work through many issues that had surfaced as a result of my time in Evin Prison, particularly my suicide attempt. Slowly but surely, this experience became less frightening for me.

I left La Ruche feeling emotionally stronger and convinced that God and time would eventually help to heal the wounds I still carried.

A few days later, Glenn and his mother were able to travel to Switzerland from South Africa. It was so amazing to see him again and talk through our prison experience together.

While I was in Switzerland, I was able to meet with an official from the United Nations who had been involved with my case. He told me that my imprisonment could not have occurred at a better time. The United Nations was hosting a six-week conference on human rights, and he was able to put considerable pressure on the Iranian delegation to get my case resolved before he was forced to bring it to the attention of the whole conference. If that occurred, other countries, particularly Germany, had indicated that their government would likely impose economic sanctions against Iran. The Iranians took the threat so seriously that one of their delegates to the conference had traveled back to Tehran twice to push for my immediate release.

As well as the political pressure, hundreds of letters had been written to the Iranian ambassador to Switzerland requesting my release.

Again I was awed at the events God had orchestrated and the people He had brought together in order to secure my freedom. Only a sovereign God could have fit all of the pieces together to effect the outcome as it had happened.

I finally arrived back in the United States on April 8, 1997.

Epilogue

I CANNOT begin to describe what it was like to arrive back home in America. All the freedoms that I had taken for granted for years were now so real. Simple freedoms, such as going for a walk, talking to family and friends, and not having to live in constant fear of being tortured or interrogated. Once I was home, I began to find out all that had been happening outside my prison cell during my incarceration. The Swiss and American governments had been working on my case daily. Three congressmen and a senator had been intimately involved in all of the negotiations, and I have had the privilege of thanking them personally for all their efforts. My release was decided by the top officials in Iran, most likely the president himself. Three weeks after arriving in prison, another American had been released from the same prison, which I didn't know about. He had been there for four and a half years; his only crime was that he was an American. Another amazing detail was that three weeks after my release, the Iranian government was indicted by the German courts for instigating the killing of some Kurdish people who had been murdered a couple of years before in a restaurant in Berlin.

This caused diplomatic relations with Europe and Iran to plummet downward. As a direct result, twenty European ambassadors to Iran, including the Swiss, were recalled back to Europe. The Swiss ambassador told me during a phone conversation to his house in Switzerland in November of 1997 that if I had been in prison just three more weeks, the Swiss would have lost all political leverage to negotiate my release, and I would have stayed in prison indefinitely. It turns out that the Swiss government spent much time trying to convince the Iranian authorities that I was Swiss. During my imprisonment, my dad would often call the Swiss embassy in Tehran and speak in the Swiss/ German language. Since all the phones were tapped, the Iranians knew that my dad was obviously Swiss, and thus in their culture I am automatically Swiss.

The tensest moment of my incarceration from the outside was when on February 26 the Swiss embassy called my parents and requested that three thousand dollars be wired immediately to pay for a lawyer for my trial. Since I had been accused of espionage, albeit falsely, I faced the death sentence if convicted. Twenty-four hours after wiring the money, my parents received another phone call from the embassy, stating that something had changed. Apparently the final trial had been canceled, and they would be able to use the money to send me back home. I believe that it was more than just the good will of the Iranian officials. I am convinced that on that night a major spiritual battle was won in the heavens. Two months after my release, a new moderate reformer was elected president of Iran: Khatameieh. He has been the main person who has brought much reform and change to Iranian society. I believe the nine weeks of intense prayer from so many Christians played a major role in his election.

All through my life, I have been very aware of the voice of God. However, there have been two specific times when His voice was so clear it was practically audible. In both instances it was a word concerning my future. The first was when I heard Him tell me that He wanted me to go as a worker for Him to Ashgabad. The second was on a December morning in 1990 when the number thirty-three came into my mind and heart. I knew something was going to happen when I was thirty-three. When I was all alone in cell fifty-eight, God brought that word back to mind, and I realized that He had prepared me for this trial. Just before my thirty-third birthday in December of 1996, right before going into Iran, I had a deep sense that Satan was going to try to kill me in the following twelve months. I thought it would be in a car accident, but once I landed in Evin Prison, I knew he would try to take my life while I was there. During my whole stay in prison, I had a deep sense that my life was in the hands of God. Halfway through my imprisonment, I felt as though God put His hands underneath me and was going to carry me out in His way and His timing, which is exactly what He did.

Since that time, I have been working with Youth With A Mission in Southern Colorado, teaching and training young people how to carry out the call God has put on their lives. Glenn got married to a girl from Germany one year later to the day from when we crossed the border from Turkmenistan into Iran. They now have a son and are working in Central Asia. Joseph Morris, the African-American I met in prison, is also out. I read in the *Denver Post* about his release, approximately nine months after mine. I have tried to locate him but have been unsuccessful.

As I look to the future, I would like to work in Asia. I also hope to return to Iran someday. I don't say that out of any sense of heroism, but out of a deep love for the Iranian people and a longing in my heart for them to know the love of God. I have met many Iranians around the world, and like those at the Frankfurt airport, they too have apologized for the actions of their government.

While I was in prison, I felt God impress on my heart that a book would be written about my story in 1999. Upon my release many people encouraged me to write a book, but I knew in my heart it wasn't the right timing. In February 1999, out of the blue, YWAM Publishing contacted me and said they had wanted to write a book about my imprisonment. I knew it was now God's timing to start the project.

I have tried to be very open and honest about my feelings during my time in prison to help let you know that I am just "Dan." But I serve an awesome God who longs to show himself faithful in all situations. God uses ordinary people. He only asks us to come and follow Him, and He will do great and mighty things in and through our lives. Matthew 14:22–29 tells the story of when Peter walked on the water. Jesus was walking on the stormy lake, and when Peter saw Him, Jesus said, "Come!" Peter then got out of the boat and started walking toward Jesus. The circumstances did not matter to Peter. All that mattered was what Jesus had said. Jesus said, "Come," so no matter how crazy it might have seemed to him and the disciples, all Peter could do was obey. As he did, he saw the glory of God and was able to do the impossible and walk on the water.

As I thought about writing this book, my heart's desire was to encourage all of us to step out of our comfort zones and walk toward Jesus. To go and do whatever He has asked, no matter what the circumstances look like. If Jesus can get me out of a high-security prison in Iran, He can deliver you from whatever situation you may be facing. Even if I would never have been released from prison, He is still Lord and is worthy of our lives. Still today, billions have yet to hear and know about Jesus. Tens of thousands of villages around the world have never heard or known this man who changed my life forever. If you have never met Him, I want to invite you to do so today. In the Bible, John 3:16 says, "For God so loved the world that he gave his one and only son that whosoever believes in him shall not perish but have eternal life." Believe and follow Jesus today, and He will forgive your sin. He will give you hope and peace and a reason to live.

For those of us who know Jesus, let us heed the admonition of Hebrews 12:1–2a. "Therefore, since we are surrounded by such a great cloud of witnesses, let us throw off everything that hinders and the sin that so easily entangles, and let us run with perseverance the race marked out for us. Let us fix our eyes on Jesus, the author and perfecter of our faith…"

1. Let us continue to fix our eyes on Jesus so that He becomes the passion of every thought, word, and deed.

2. Let us continue to pray for the Muslim world so that the love and knowledge of Jesus are made known to everyone and that all the powers of Satan are destroyed.

3. Finally, let us go and preach the Good News to everyone. Let each of us take our responsibility and privilege seriously to fulfill the Great Commission and see God worshiped on the earth.

For more information on Dan Baumann or to arrange a speaking engagement, e-mail 103266.2451@compuserve.com.

❧, ❧, ❧, ❧

Dan Baumann is presently serving with Youth With A Mission at YWAM Trinidad, Colorado. This base is dedicated to discipling young people, to church planting in Trinidad, and to seeing God worshiped in the nations of the earth. The Rocky Mountain Discipleship Training School is a five-month training program with three months of training and a two-month outreach to the 10/40 Window. If you would like more information,

CALL
719-868-2700

OR E-MAIL
ywam@ywamcolorado.org

OR VISIT OUR WEBSITE AT
www.ywamcolorado.org

Dan at the Swiss ambassador's residence on March 16, 1997, the day of his release from prison.

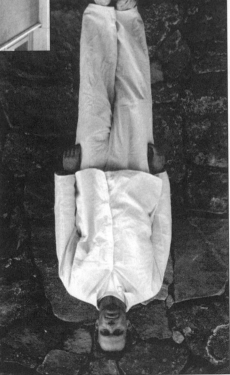

Dan in a replica of his prison clothes.